The Gambler

The Gambler

Tallulah Sharpe

LIBRIS

An *X Libris* Book

First published by X Libris in 1996

A CIP catalogue for this book
is available from the British Library.

ISBN 0 7515 1690 2

Photoset in North Wales by
Derek Doyle & Associates, Mold, Clwyd
Printed and bound in Great Britain by
Clays Ltd, St Ives plc

X Libris
A Division of
Little, Brown and Company (UK)
Brettenham House
Lancaster Place
London WC2E 7EN

The Gambler

Chapter One

SAM WINTERTON IMPATIENTLY tapped on the desk with her pencil. Glancing across to the international clocks she saw that it was still only four p.m. in New York. A worried look spread across her face as she thought about her imminent redundancy and the financial problems it would soon cause. On top of this she was losing Tobias, her boss and lover.

As thoughts of Toby entered her mind she looked over to watch him through the glass partition between their offices. Toby was hunched over his desk, packing up the last of his personal effects. Suddenly aware of her gaze, he looked up and smiled. After all this time, that smile could still make her stomach churn with excitement. Even from this distance she could see the lines crinkle around his green eyes. He shrugged his shoulders, as if to say, 'I know how you're feeling.'

Sam felt frustration seep through her. This was to be their last few hours together before his flight to Tokyo where a new job, new life and no doubt

1

new lovers were waiting for him. He'd be finished packing soon and ready for her but she still had to wait for the New York phone call. She also needed a new job, a new life. Over fifty brokers and dealers at Walker, Rathbone were being made redundant and they were all as desperate as her to get a new position. She had got used to life on a high salary – a large apartment overlooking the Thames, a Porsche and expensive holidays – and she didn't want to give it all up now. And like Toby, she had decided that nowhere was too far to go in order to keep that lifestyle.

The screens around the office flickered with financial news from across the globe. Sam perused the screen in a desultory fashion. Did she really want a similar job? At times her work seemed sterile and worthless, but after five years in the business she really couldn't see what else she could do. And even if she did take another job in finance, she sadly doubted that she would ever meet another lover as good as Toby. He did things to her body that she hadn't experienced or even imagined before and, as she wryly admitted to herself, at twenty-eight, she certainly knew her way around a bedroom.

For Toby, the solution to both of her problems was easy – why not go to Japan with him? Part of her wanted to desperately, but the sensible, practical side of her was worried that she'd never find a job there and would end up being no more than an appendage to him, an attractive escort to impress all his new business friends. A geisha girl. He had angrily denied this, of course. But Sam knew that if she couldn't work she could only justify her existence there by becoming the perfect accessory.

'You want to powder your nose?'

Sam was jolted out of her thoughts by her friend's face looming over her own. 'Judy! Where did you spring from? It's nine o'clock – haven't you got a home to go to?'

Judy laughed. 'I could say the same for you.'

The remark hit on a nerve. For all the expensive and beautiful artefacts that adorned Sam's flat, it didn't feel like a home at all. Sometimes it seemed no more than a cold, empty shell, and now it would be worse. Now that Toby's hastily discarded clothes would no longer mark a trail across the floor towards her bedroom, now that her sheets would no longer smell of his musky scent, now that she would no longer wake in the mornings to find herself held in his arms, still drenched in sweat from their lovemaking . . .

Judy sensed her distraction. 'Are you okay?'

'Sorry, Judy. I'm expecting a call from America and Toby's off soon. He's flying out tonight.'

'Oh, hon, I forgot. C'mon, I want a love update.'

Sam had become firm friends with Judy from the moment she started at Walker, Rathbone. Their 'love updates' in the ladies' toilets had become something of a ritual. Judy would always bang on the door of each cubicle to check they were alone before launching into a hilarious conversation about the latest office scandal or the desperate state of her own love life.

As Judy led the way past Toby's office, Sam looked in, but he was on the phone, oblivious to her. She followed her friend into the ladies' and they installed themselves in front of the mirror.

3

Judy looked with disgust at the bright fluorescent light. 'Why do they insist on this type of lighting in ladies' loos? It does nothing for a woman's complexion. Although,' she said admiringly, 'yours looks good under any light.'

'You always say that and it's not true,' replied Sam, looking at herself in the mirror. Her wide blue eyes seemed tired and in contrast to her long black hair her skin, usually pale, looked ashen under the harsh artificial light. According to Toby she had a cute nose and the most sensuous lips he had ever kissed. Who would kiss them now? she wondered, straightening her new jacket and undoing the top button of her blue silk blouse.

Judy squirted some gel into her hand and ran it through her bottle-blonde cropped hair. She studied her reflection and scowled. Judy was six years older than Sam, six long hard years, as she insisted on saying, though underneath her thick make-up, she was still a good-looking woman. Still single on her thirtieth birthday, she had woken up, decided that desperate times called for desperate measures, reached for the peroxide and turned herself into, in her words, 'Supertramp'.

'So what're your plans for your last couple of hours of lust?' Judy asked, reapplying her trademark scarlet lipstick.

'At this rate, I'll be lucky if I get more than a peck on the cheek. I'm never going to get out of the office. I've been waiting all day for a response from a firm in New York. Toby or no Toby, in a week's time I'll be collecting my P45.'

Judy patted her friend on the shoulder. 'You're a fantastic broker. You're bound to find work soon.'

'Me and a few thousand others.' Sam sighed. 'Look, I'd better get back. I can't miss that call. I'll speak to you tomorrow.'

'It'll work out okay, hon,' said Judy, looking in the mirror and checking her teeth for lipstick.

As they came out of the toilets, Sam could hear the phone ringing in her office. She said a quick goodbye to Judy and rushed back to her desk to pick it up. 'Hello?' she said breathlessly.

'Hello. This is Mr Stein's office in New York. Is that Ms Winterton?'

Sam felt relieved: the sooner she sorted out New York the sooner she and Toby could be together. And of course, there was the prospect of a job, though right now, that seemed less important. Before she could answer the question, the secretary informed her that Mr Stein wouldn't be in the office for another hour.

Sam tried to keep the impatience out of her voice. 'Could you make sure he rings me as soon as he gets in. Please.'

'Sure will, ma'am. Have a nice day.'

For a moment, Sam forgot about Toby as she wondered if she'd ever be able to handle America if she had to listen to people constantly ordering her to 'have a nice day.' Then she caught sight of her lover, still on the telephone, and her heart sank. She loved watching him talk. Although she couldn't hear him through the glass, his face was so expressive she could practically tell what the conversation was about. It amazed Sam the way Toby's hands never stopped moving as he spoke. With a phone in one hand, the other seemed to work twice as hard, waving in the air to emphasise a point or smoothing his blond hair back from his face. The sleeves of his shirt were rolled back and she could see the muscles on his forearm tensing as he punctuated his conversation with gestures.

Sam thought about those hands on her, the frantic way they investigated her body in bed, searching for new places to touch her, almost desperate, as if each time he touched her it would be the last. And now, of course, it would be the last time.

For what seemed like forever, she busied herself finishing off a client's report which had lain untouched on her desk since the announcement of her impending redundancy. She had no heart for the job anymore. Although the prospect of unemployment scared her, she felt almost glad to be leaving. She couldn't imagine what it would be like to sit at her desk, looking across at Toby's office and not to see him there, blowing her kisses when no-one was looking or smiling his reassuring smile when she looked stressed out.

The phone rang again. Sam picked it up on the second ring. This has to be it, she prayed. She could hear from the crackle on the line that it was long distance.

'Hi Sam, it's Steve, New York,' the caller drawled.

'Mr Stein?'

'Yeah. I got your message and I'm looking into it but I need some more details.'

As she concentrated on Stein's questions, she didn't see Toby come up behind her. He slid his arms around her and kissed the top of her head. She took a deep breath, savouring the odour of

6

his body. Judy had once described his smell as 'all testosterone and Obsession For Men'.

'What kinda salary were you thinking of, Sam?'

'I'm on fifty thousand here.'

The telephone conversation continued with Toby massaging her shoulders as she tried to convince Steve Stein that she was the woman for the job. Every so often Toby would lean over and gently bite her earlobes and then run his tongue down her neck. Half-heartedly she pushed him away, signalling to him that this call was important but secretly hoping he wouldn't take her at her word.

'Sure, Steve, I understand that.' Stop it, she mouthed at Toby, smiling.

Toby took no notice and began to undo her jacket. Sam slapped his hands away but they came back, more forcefully this time. While she awkwardly switched the phone from one hand to the other, he removed her jacket and then began unbuttoning her blouse. At first she resisted but, worried that he might just rip it off her completely, she resigned herself to her delicious fate. Toby expertly flicked the last pearl button and her blouse fell open, revealing her round breasts pushed up over her bra, their whiteness given an eerie blue glow by the terminal flashing in front of her.

She felt herself being gently propelled forward as Toby's thumbs slid under her bra straps and pulled them off her shoulders. As he marked out a trail of kisses along her collarbone, his hot, powerful hands dipped into her bra and freed her breasts. Cupping them, he thumbed her nipples which were already stiffening with excitement.

Sam placed her hand over his, forcing Toby to squeeze her breasts.

'If there did happen to be a vacancy, how soon do you think you'd be able to start?' asked Steve.

'Straight away,' she said, letting out a little gasp as Toby thumbed her nipples.

'I'd like you to have a quick word with my boss, just to help things along.'

Sam wasn't prepared for this turn of events. She couldn't say no but she didn't want to say no to Toby either. 'Great,' she said, trying to sound enthusiastic. She put her mouth over the handpiece and said, 'Just give me five minutes. Please.'

He let go of her breasts and turned her chair around to face him. 'No,' he laughed, dropping to his knees. Crouching in front of her, he started licking her breasts, his tongue circling her areolas. Sam had a hard head for business but at this precise moment she felt that allowing Toby to do his worst was almost worth all the dollars she could earn in the future. Almost – but not quite.

She playfully slapped Toby's head away but this only seemed to inflame his desire. He brushed her hands aside and returned to her breasts with renewed vigour, moving from nipple to nipple, taking each into his mouth, moistening them then blowing on them, making her shiver.

Thankfully, there was still nobody at the other end of the line so, cradling the phone, Sam pulled Toby's face up to meet hers and kissed his eyelids. Then, playfully biting his nose, she let her mouth slide down to meet his, loving the way the firmness of his lips echoed the hardness of his body. She wanted him so much.

8

As Toby slid his tongue deep into her mouth, making her flesh erupt in goose pimples, the line suddenly clicked.

'Ms Winterton, it's Pete Brown here, how do you do.'

Sam tried to deflect Toby's advances. 'Fine, thank you. Of course, I'd feel a lot better if I knew you had work to offer me,' she said, laughing. And if I could just get back to Toby's lips, she thought.

She heard her voice echoing squeakily across the Atlantic. After several seconds of silence, Peter Brown's reply came back, and Sam watched as Toby manoeuvred himself between her legs. He licked her stomach and she could feel the faint stubble on his chin grazing against her belly. His tongue investigated her navel then dipped beneath the waistband of her skirt. Obviously frustrated by the way the material impeded his progress, Toby then grabbed hold of her knees and prised her legs apart, hiking her short, black skirt up to her hips.

Sam sat back in her chair and for several minutes Toby just gazed at her, admiring her long, slim legs. In preparation for this moment she had put on her sexiest underwear, sheer black stockings and suspenders and a pair of lacy black knickers which Toby had bought for her after their first night together.

'Wider,' mouthed Toby, and Sam obliged. He then began to work his way up her thighs, biting and kissing as he went. 'You taste great,' he whispered, as he licked a line towards her crotch.

Sam thought she would break as Toby grabbed hold of her knees and spread her legs even further to allow him to move closer to his target. He pressed his face against her crotch and inhaled, savouring her smell, then licked the pretty material that shielded her sex. But her knickers offered little protection from his probing tongue and Sam had to stifle a moan as she felt the filmy lace become drenched in the wetness of his mouth. Almost involuntarily she thrust her pelvis into his face, now overwhelmed by the need to feel his tongue on her clitoris, on her lips and pushing hard inside her.

Peter Brown droned on, asking her the same questions Steve Stein had put to her only minutes before, and Sam prayed that her irregular breathing and startled gasps would be put down to the international telephone system. When Toby yanked her legs up over his shoulders and ripped her knickers to one side, tearing the delicate fabric, she knew that she would have to wind up the phone call fast.

'Peter, something's come up here. Can I call you back?'

Sam watched as Toby stared at her glistening lips and she felt her clitoris throbbing for attention. He bent his head forward, licking at the tidy patch of black hair on her pubis, then slowly, ever so slowly, he moved down until his face nuzzled into her soaking wet vagina. His expert tongue separated the folds of her labia as he moved closer to the hard nub of flesh at the centre of her pleasure.

'Sure, Peter, that'll be great,' she said, throwing the phone down on to her desk. By now she had decided that it was tough if she lost the job. Some things were more important.

With both hands she grabbed Toby's head and shoved his face against her pubis. There was no other man in the world who knew how to use his mouth as well as Toby. One moment he would gently suck on her clit, the next his tongue would plough into her ferociously, making her whole body quiver. As his snake-like tongue explored the softness inside her, Sam grabbed his hair and rubbed her clitoris against his nose, uncertain for how long she'd be able to hold back.

Sensing her approaching orgasm, Toby moved away and lifted her legs off his shoulders. He held her by the calves, causing her labia to spread, revealing her dark wet orifice, and she watched the look of desire on his face as he savoured the sight before him. His hands moved up her legs, and as his nails dug into her thighs, she slid her fingers deep into her moist vagina, then moved on to her clitoris. Sam began stroking the pink bud, knowing that it would drive Toby wild, and she glanced down to see an appreciative bulge pulse in his trousers.

For a moment she was content to masturbate for him, her hand just a sensual blur of activity between her outstretched thighs. But though the sensations jolted her body, it wasn't enough. She wanted, needed him, needed his cock. Quickly, she undid his zip while he leaned on her legs, opening her up ever deeper. To Sam the swelling in Toby's boxer shorts looked painfully trapped and she dragged the waistband down around his solid thighs letting his stiffened penis spring out into the air. With one hand she cupped his balls while gently rubbing the head of his cock with the other. His foreskin felt silky and delicate in

11

comparison to the hardness underneath. Toby let out a groan, his breathing becoming heavier, and he relinquished his hold of her legs, making her kneel in front of him.

Sam didn't release her grip for a second, even when he grabbed her head and thrust his cock into her mouth, its size stretching her lips to their limits. She licked around the head, running her tongue under his foreskin, tasting the salt of his pre-come, and Toby groaned louder. His thrusting grew more insistent, forcing his rigid member far into her mouth until her nose grazed against his wiry blond pubic hair and she could smell his strong, masculine musk. His cock reached the back of her throat but Sam ignored the pain this caused, wanting him ever further inside her.

When Toby withdrew on the verge of orgasm, she grabbed hold of his tight, compact balls and tugged him towards her. 'Please come. Come in my mouth.'

Toby just grunted and rubbed his penis around her face, leaving traces of his juices on her cheeks.

'Please, please come,' Sam begged.

But Toby wasn't ready to end it yet. He dragged Sam to her feet and with one sweep of his arm cleared her desk, sending files and coffee cups flying and knocking her phone on to the floor where it trilled briefly then went dead. Face forward he bent Sam over the desk, hiked her skirt high over her bottom and tore away the remaining shreds of her knickers.

At first he just rubbed his hand gently over her milky white behind, teasing her by running his fingers down her cleft.

'Fuck me now, you bastard, or I'm going to explode,' she pleaded.

Toby laughed, and worked two fingers inside her, building up a rhythm he knew would make her frantic. Sam gyrated her hips towards him, grinding her buttocks into his crotch and feeling the wet head of his penis slipping, sliding against her cheeks. Toby's cock throbbed as angrily as her clitoris, its veins bulging from the surging of his blood, and Sam could tell that, like her, he couldn't take much more of this procrastination.

Toby removed his fingers and in one rapid movement plunged his manhood into her aching vagina. Holding on to her hair, he squashed her face against the desk, fucking her hard and fast. Sam began frantically rubbing her clitoris, knowing that she was about to come, and from the quickening of his thrusts, she sensed that Toby was too.

'I'm going to come,' she gasped and as she finished the sentence her sex started to pulsate, her juices drenching Toby's cock.

'Yeah, oh yeah. Now!' shouted Toby.

Sam felt the warm spurts shoot deep inside her and her vagina contracted, gripping his cock tighter and tighter. Waves of pleasure erupted from between her legs, the sensation swelling and rushing through her body with an intensity that made her feel faint.

Toby collapsed on top of her and for a moment they lay helpless on the desk, he kissing the back of her neck while she panted, trying to catch her breath. When both of their orgasms finally subsided, they couldn't help but look up at the clock. It had gone ten.

Toby kissed her long and hard and then sat down on her chair with a sigh. 'I'm going to have to go in a minute.'

Sam rearranged her clothing while mentally she tried to compose her emotions. But Toby's next remark knocked her back again.

'Please come with me. I'll take care of you.'

She looked into his eyes and could see his pain. She was tempted, but so much could go wrong. She could end up in a strange country with no job and a lover who regretted that he'd pleaded with her to accompany him. Sam had been in that position before and the humiliation had stayed with her. She would never again put a man above all else.

She took a deep breath. 'I'll keep on applying for jobs over there but I'm not coming over without one. On the other hand, you could always stay here and be a house husband.'

'Touché.'

'Can I give you a lift to the airport?' she asked, changing the subject.

'I can't stand emotional goodbyes at airports. Let's just do it here.' Toby stood up to get dressed, his expression set and determined.

A shiver of fear ran through her. Toby was shutting down and in a few minutes it would be as if the last half hour had never happened. Sam was always amazed at the ability men had to compartmentalise their lives and their feelings. But she hadn't lived this long without learning to mimic their behaviour. Picking up the mess on the floor, she said, 'Perhaps that's for the best, I have to ring New York back anyway.'

Toby looked hurt by her tone and Sam reflected

14

that all men, Toby included, were hypocrites. It was one rule for them and another for the little woman. She knew that she was using anger to hide her pain, but it didn't stop her dismissing Toby with a curt, 'You'd better finish your packing.'

She dialled Peter Brown's number.

'Peter Brown's office. How can I help you?'

'Is Mr Brown there? It's Ms Winterton.'

'I'm sorry, he's had to leave for a meeting down town. He won't be back today.'

'Oh, okay. I'll call tomorrow.'

She replaced the handset before the receptionist had a chance to reply. No, she wouldn't have a nice day.

Toby reappeared in her doorway. 'I guess it's time to say goodbye.' He walked towards her.

Sam cleared her throat, trying to hide the emotion in her voice. 'I'll really miss you.'

'I'll call you as soon as I get there. If you change your mind . . .'

Sam interrupted him. 'I won't. Take care of yourself and have a safe journey.' She hated herself for sounding so matter of fact but she didn't know what else to say, or rather, she had no words that could make either of them feel any better.

Toby leaned forward and gave her a great bear hug and for an instant she felt like caving in and accepting his protection. Instead, she kissed him on each cheek. 'Au revoir. Don't do anything I wouldn't do.'

'As if,' he said and with a slight shrug he turned and walked out of the office.

As soon as Sam knew he had left the building she sat down and wept.

Chapter Two

SAM PACED UP and down her bedroom, her head spinning as she wondered why Toby hadn't called in a fortnight. Her most charitable explanation had him lying seriously ill, either in his rented flat or some high-tech Japanese hospital. This would explain, she told herself, why she could only get his answerphone. Not that she understood what the Japanese voice was saying. Perhaps it wasn't even his answerphone.

Less charitably she pictured him being entertained by beautiful Japanese women whose only job was to satisfy his every whim and desire. Her imagination went into overdrive as she thought of him lying naked and acquiescent on a bed, being anointed with massage oils, the blond hair on his thighs glistening as the expert hands moved up and down his strong, taut leg muscles. In her mind's eye, she saw how his cock twitched as the many hands moved closer to his scrotum. She saw the desire on his face as his testicles were lightly touched and teased by the gentle fingers. Sam knew from her own experience that this would drive him into a frenzy.

The picture moved on. As Toby's cock rose to a full erection, one of the women, helped by the others, slowly took off her kimono to reveal that she was completely naked underneath. Her body was perfect. Her breasts were small and round, the nipples dark brown and erect. Her black pubic hair was shaved in an exact triangle but the lips of her vulva could barely be seen. By now Toby was begging for her to sit on him. The woman laughed as she bent her head down and teased his cock with her tongue. The other women continued to massage him.

The women looked at each other and nodded as if to say they thought he was ready. The naked woman rose from the bed and in one graceful movement straddled Toby's stomach. Opening his eyes he looked up between her legs. He could just see the wetness within her neat brown labia. The lips were slightly open, ready and waiting for him.

'Please,' he gasped.

The woman slowly bent her knees until she was hovering just above his member. Her lips teased the head of his cock, leaving traces of her moisture. Suddenly Toby grabbed the woman's hips and brought her down on to him, letting out a sigh of relief as his cock filled her up. She was so light, he could easily lift her up and down as he thrust into her, harder and faster, until he came.

A phone rang. Sam found herself on her bed and, to her surprise, she was masturbating. Tears filled her eyes as she got up and picked up the phone on the desk, shaking her head as if to dispel these obsessive thoughts about Toby. She looked angrily at her blank computer screen. Its silence seemed a direct criticism of her.

'Hi, it's Judy. I'm just making sure you're not being a lady of leisure and still lying in bed.'

Sam felt embarrassed at having been caught out. 'Very funny,' she said, a little too sharply. 'The last place I want to be at the moment is in bed, on my own, thinking about absent friends and wondering if I'm ever going to get another job.'

Judy apologised. 'I'm so thoughtless.'

'It's not your fault, Jude. I'm just having a bad morning. I can't even begin to tell you what I've been imagining Toby's up to. Why hasn't he called me?'

There was a silence on the other end of the line.

'Look, if even you can't offer me words of comfort I'm doomed.'

'Maybe he's been sent away or something.' Judy didn't sound very convincing.

'To a place where they have no phones?' There was a bitterness creeping into Sam's voice.

'Okay, he's a typical man. He promises you everything and delivers nothing. Just like all the others. Let's not talk about him any more. What's happening on the job front?'

'Sweet FA. The New York job didn't come off. At this rate I won't be able to pay the phone bill to cover the cost of all the calls I've made.' Sam knew this was an exaggeration but she didn't feel like keeping a stiff upper lip.

'Something'll turn up. I'm not just saying that,' Judy said quickly.

'Let's meet for lunch, Thursday, usual place. You can pay.'

'Great. Sam, I'm going to have to go. The other line's ringing.'

Sam put down the phone.

'Get a grip on yourself, girl,' she said out loud to herself.

She would start by tidying up the flat, beginning with her bedroom. She drew back the cream hessian curtains to reveal one of her main reasons for buying the place – the view. In front of her lay the majestic sight of Tower Bridge and the dark, murky waters of the Thames flowing beneath it. She never got bored of the view, whatever the weather or time of day. It was a vista that constantly changed. An added bonus was that she wasn't overlooked. She could stand there naked, as she did now, and nobody could see. It gave her a sense of freedom that she felt most people in London were denied. But today, even this couldn't calm her. Instead, she found herself thinking that she would have to default on the mortgage if she didn't get a job soon. She saw herself featuring as a tabloid headline. Another yuppie falling on hard times and losing their dream home.

Keep busy, she told herself. She turned away from the window and faced the bed. Was it really only four months ago that Toby had helped her choose the antique wrought-iron bedstead? It was back in the spring, when they'd been together for only a couple of weeks. Most of that time had been spent in her old bed and it had taken something of a pounding. She had wanted a new one to celebrate this new relationship, so one Sunday morning, the two of them had managed to put their lovemaking on hold long enough to go hunting around the antique shops in Greenwich. Finding the bed she had wanted, she had blushed furiously as Toby blurted out to the dealer that the posts were ideal for tying Sam's hands to. But it wasn't only her cheeks that had burned.

Sam had been excited by the endless erotic possibilities that this new relationship promised. She'd had many lovers prior to Toby and had been somewhat disappointed by all of them. Most of the men she had dated previously had been staid and conservative in their attitudes to sex, to the point that sometimes she felt that maybe there was something wrong with her sexually, always wanting more, wanting something different. Then Toby came along and made her feel good about her fantasies. He made her write a list of everything she'd ever dreamed of doing and pinned it to the fridge. He'd sworn they would do everything, in time.

But there wasn't time. Toby had gone and she tried not to think about that sad reminder still in her kitchen. Straightening the cream broderie anglaise counterpane on her bed she considered throwing the list away. But she couldn't bring herself to do it. Not yet. Keeping it was keeping hold of Toby.

She looked around the room to see if there was anything else she could tidy. This tidying therapy was of limited use when you were a compulsively neat person with only the minimum of furniture. The bedroom's off-white walls were bare, apart from a large, French-style mirror opposite the bed. Again, Sam couldn't control herself and her mind strayed to the many nights she and Toby had delighted in watching themselves make love in the mirror.

Her favourite position had been with Toby taking her from behind at an angle to the mirror which allowed them to see each thrust he made. Before Toby entered her he would gently part her buttocks so she could see her labia opening up like a flower, a carefully positioned lamp illuminating every fold of her flesh. Toby would run his finger softly down the edges of her lips and then move on to her clitoris while his thumb teased around the wet opening.

Sam always wriggled into the right position to allow Toby's thumb to push inside her, while his finger played with her clit and his hard cock grazed against her buttocks. Taking his hand away, Toby would spread her buttocks even further apart so she could see his cock in all its glory as it entered her. He would always do this slowly so that she could savour every inch as it disappeared.

Why couldn't she just stop thinking about him? It was over. Her silk dressing gown lay on the ink-blue chaise longue and she absent-mindedly picked it up and hung it in her wardrobe before crossing the room to the tallboy and reaching into a drawer for some underwear. She didn't dare even to begin to think about the sexual associations of the mound of lace and silk. With a quick glance she saw that her desk in the far corner was meticulous.

Sam knew there was no point in investigating the state of her galley kitchen. The high-tech metal surfaces were always pristine, good enough to eat off – or fuck on, as Toby had proved on more than one occasion. And the list would be there, forcing her to acknowledge what had been taken away from her. Damn him, she thought, as she walked into the living room.

Perhaps she could use this spare time to decorate the flat? It was no good trying to convince herself that this parting was just as hard on Toby. Everything must be new and exciting to him in Japan. Nothing had changed for her and that sameness caused her to feel his absence all the more strongly. Maybe if she decorated, she could paint him out of her life.

She looked around her. The walls in the living room, like everywhere else, were painted an off-white, matching the plump sofas and the raffia flooring. The walls were just a background to her collection of black-and-white photographs. She loved their clean, unobtrusive aestheticism. Bright colours had always seemed too intrusive, too demanding of attention.

By the sofa, which faced a large-screen television, lay the remains of her microwave dinner for one: the only thing out of place in the room and yet another sad reminder of her present condition. She picked up the plate at once and deposited the remains in the kitchen bin, then put plate into the dishwasher, carefully avoiding looking at the piece of paper on the refrigerator door.

The phone rang again but Sam had gone past the point of thinking the caller would be either Toby or a job offer. 'Hello,' she said tonelessly.

'Sam?'

'Yes.'

It was a man's voice but not Toby's. 'It's Marcus.'

Marcus! She couldn't believe it.

Shortly after starting at Walker, Rathbone, Sam was given the task of managing a small part of Marcus McLeod's vast portfolio. Marcus was one of the company's biggest clients – but not, as it quickly became clear, one of their most prized. Walker, Rathbone was an old and very traditional company and there was always great embarrassment over their involvement with Marcus. He was a self-made multi-millionaire, notorious in the City for his huge appetite for gambling, matched only by his taste for women. Scandal followed him around and he was rarely out of the newspapers. His money was too important to the company for them to refuse to manage it, but none of the more senior brokers would have anything to do with his investments. And so the job always fell to newcomers like Sam.

On taking up her new task, she nervously phoned Marcus to arrange a meeting to discuss his requirements. Barely minutes into the call, he invited her out to dinner and much to her own amazement she said yes. Judy overheard and dragged Sam off to the toilets for the first of their many love updates.

'What on earth do you think you're doing?' asked Judy, shocked. 'Surely you've heard of Marcus McLeod?'

'Of course I have. It's just a business meeting,' replied Sam, unsure if she believed this herself.

'That man has no concept of separating business from pleasure. Take it from one who's seen both his spreadsheets and his bed sheets, so to speak.'

'You've slept with him!' Sam laughed. 'What was he like?'

'Shh!' whispered Judy, as another broker entered the toilets. 'I'll tell you about it another time. It wasn't something I'm particularly proud of. The man has had every woman in the Square Mile.'

'Not every woman,' replied Sam defiantly.

Later, looking at Marcus McLeod across a candlelit table, Sam wasn't sure how long her defiance would hold out. He was gorgeous. In his early forties, with dark hair slightly peppered with grey, he was dressed in a sober handmade suit, an immaculate white shirt and a muted tie. His face was slightly lined, something which perversely seemed to make him all the more handsome.

Contrary to her expectations, the talk over the meal was kept strictly to business. She watched him as he took care of the bill and left to keep another appointment, and wondered what she had done wrong.

The answer was nothing. The next day, flowers were delivered to her office with a note from Marcus thanking her for being such a charming dinner companion. It was the beginning of a good period in Sam's life. Marcus delighted in her astute management of his money and the company too were impressed by her acumen. Her private life also blossomed as she and Marcus embarked on what was to all intents and purposes an affair. It certainly had all the ingredients of an affair. Everything, that was, bar sex. Marcus had never asked her to go to bed with him. Sometimes this caused an unbearable

24

tension inside Sam and finally, driving back from yet another chaste weekend away in the country, Sam cracked. 'What's wrong with me, Marcus?'

He knew exactly what she was talking about. 'Nothing. Nothing at all.'

'Then why won't you sleep with me?'

He kept his eye on the road, driving in silence, refusing to answer the question.

'Why, Marcus?'

He turned to her and his answer made her all the more confused. 'Because I'm in love with you.'

This admission drove a wedge between them. Sam bitterly regretted asking him that question but the ache in her had grown too strong to keep silent. She loved him too, which to her made it all the more ludicrous that they'd never made love.

Although Marcus wouldn't be drawn on the subject again, Sam tried to piece together the possible reasons for his refusal to consummate their relationship. Obviously he had no problems sexually as any number of women she knew were willing to testify. But as his track record had shown, he seemed to be suffering from a fear of commitment. And yet he was always willing to see Sam, to let their relationship develop. So why wouldn't he sleep with her?

Sam was never to find out. Shortly after that conversation, a huge scandal exploded. In the newspapers, accusations were made against Marcus of insider dealing, although from the areas of his finances that she had dealt with, there had never been any hint of anything untoward. As the scandal threatened to engulf Walker, Rathbone, they had no option but to cease trading on Marcus's behalf. One morning, Sam awoke to find a group of reporters camping outside her house wanting to know more about her relationship with the rogue millionaire. She felt forced to go out and make a statement to them – a terse 'no comment'. After all, she truly knew nothing.

That same day a note arrived from Marcus which said a simple goodbye and apologised for dragging her name through the mud. As far as she was aware, Marcus had then slipped quietly out of the country and into hiding. It had hurt at the time, but as the months passed, the memory of him faded and then she had met Toby, who had been poached from a rival of Walker, Rathbone at great cost. Toby, who had seemed so much like Marcus. Until it came to the bedroom . . .

'Sam?'

Sam shook her head. 'Marcus, sorry. It's just that this is a little out of the blue.'

'How are you, Sam? It's been a long time.'

'Marcus, you've caught me at a bad moment. Why don't you give me a ring in a week or so and I might feel a bit more willing to take a stroll down memory lane with you,' she said, making no attempt to hide the bitterness in her voice. She felt emotionally vulnerable and had no wish to give Marcus the chance to exploit her insecurity.

'Are you still angry with me?' He laughed as he asked the question, but he wasn't mocking her.

'After all these years? You're overrating your own importance.' Sam wasn't going to budge an inch.

'You're angry about something. Is it about losing your job? Or is it Toby?'

At the mention of Toby's name, Sam burst into angry tears.

Marcus was quiet for a while and then in a comforting tone said, 'It hurts me hearing you like this, Sam. I want to make things right between us.'

Sam choked back a sob. 'How do you know so much about my life?'

'You know what a close watch I keep over all my affairs.'

'My life hasn't been your affair for a long time.'

'Oh, but it has, Sam. And that's why I'm here now. I've got a proposition which I hope will solve all your problems.'

Sam composed herself. It was time to let her head rule over her heart. If Marcus had a job for her, she'd take it, even if he was only offering it to her out of sympathy. Indulging in her emotions was a luxury she could no longer afford.

She cleared her throat. 'And this proposition is?'

'When have I ever done business with you over the phone? I'll see you at my club on the twenty-fifth at eight o'clock.'

The line cleared and Sam felt better than she had in a long time.

As she entered Marcus's club Sam told herself that she wasn't going to get caught up in any of his game playing. This was going to be strictly business. But as the heavy oak door closed behind her and she caught the smell of old leather armchairs, old men and too many cigars, she was instantly transported back to their first meeting there and remembered that she'd told herself exactly the same thing back then.

She waited at the reception feeling uncomfortable in the all-male environment. The club had been shaken to its foundations when its members had been forced to accept that, as they neared the end of the twentieth century, they should, perhaps, allow in women guests. The motion had been carried by only five votes and the mostly ancient members blamed it on 'young upstarts' like Marcus.

'Mr McLeod is waiting for you in the Wellington Room, madam,' wheezed the arthritic-looking old man behind the reception desk.

Sam nodded at him, then strode through the club looking purposeful, ignoring the glares she was getting from all quarters. The old buzzards might have had to accept the majority's decision but it didn't mean they had to like it.

Marcus rose from his chair and kissed her on each cheek.

'Sit down. You look great.'

And you too, Marcus, she thought. In fact he was looking better than ever. 'Thanks,' she said, nervously tugging at her skirt which she decided was much too short for the occasion.

Marcus glanced down at her legs admiringly. 'Would you like some champagne?'

Without waiting for her reply, he clicked his fingers. A man dressed in a butler's uniform straight out of the twenties sidled across the room and Marcus whispered in his ear.

Five minutes later Marcus was clinking his glass against Sam's. 'To our future partnership.'

She was aware that every man in the room was looking at them. 'I think we're being watched,' she laughed.

'I don't think the old duffers like the fact that a reprobate like me was allowed to keep my membership.' Marcus lifted his glass and nodded to the onlookers who scowled at him, then hid behind their newspapers. 'They've never forgiven me for the fact that nothing was proved.'

'Marcus, what did happen?' Damn it. She had promised herself that she wasn't going to bring up the past.

'I think a lot of people thought that I was getting a little bit above myself – a working-class boy who hadn't paid his dues, that sort of thing. A whispering campaign started. You know how it is.'

Thankfully, he was gracious enough to pretend that they were both talking about the financial scandal. Sam didn't want any messy emotionalism getting in the way of the business in hand. And despite all the intervening years and the hurt she had gone through, getting emotional around Marcus would still be so easy. She drained her champagne and just smiled, waiting for him to bring up the reason for this meeting.

Marcus refilled her glass and gazed at her thoughtfully. 'You've grown into your beauty, Sam. In my absence you've become a woman.'

This is not what I want to hear, she thought, blushing furiously. His intimacy unnerved her. 'About this proposition . . .'

'Ah, yes. Business.' Marcus was playing with her.

'Do you want me to handle some share deals?' she asked abruptly.

Marcus laughed. 'Oh, nothing like that. I was thinking of a much more intimate relationship.'

The champagne had gone to her head and she was having trouble collecting her thoughts. 'I think we've been here before, Marcus. It wasn't a great success and, to be honest, it doesn't pay the bills.'

'This time it'll be different. What I'm proposing could make you a very rich woman.'

Sam waited for him to continue.

'Now, as you know, my greatest passion is gambling, whether on the stock exchange or at a roulette table. But lately, it's grown a bit stale and I'd like to add a new frisson.'

'Go on.'

'I want you to gamble with me. Well, actually, gamble against me. I'll give you twenty thousand to start with and whatever you win you keep. Better than a nine to five job any day, don't you think?'

'What's the catch?'

'If you lose you have to pay a forfeit.'

'Which is?'

Marcus looked her straight in the eye and said, in all seriousness, 'You must have sex with a person or people of my choice. And I must be allowed to watch.'

It took several minutes for Sam to take in what he had said. Was he mad? From the outraged coughs and the rustling of newspapers, she could tell that most of the men in the room had overheard their conversation. Before she could voice her thoughts Marcus took out a videotape from his briefcase.

'Before you give your answer watch this. It

should give you some idea of what the position entails. Then when you've made up your mind, call me. The offer is open for exactly twenty-four hours.'

Sam stared at him, open-mouthed. She wanted to say so much but she knew he had ended the conversation. He finished the last of the champagne and stood. 'Speak to you soon,' he said as he left.

Sam put down her drink and followed behind. Outside, Marcus was nowhere to be seen. She hailed a cab. She wanted to get home as fast as possible to think about what had happened. And watch the tape.

Chapter Three

SAM'S TELEVISION CAME to life with a woman and man facing each other across the bed in what was obviously Marcus's bedroom. Although she had never actually been to his home, Sam had seen it featured once in *Interiors*. She didn't recognise the couple. The woman was facing the camera wearing only her white underwear. She had a short, blonde bob, heavy eye make-up and red, full lips. Sam admired her large breasts, small waist and plump hips, envious of the woman's figure compared to her own, more boyish shape.

The man, only an inch or two taller than the woman, was also stripped down to his underwear, which clung tight around his firm buttocks. Italian-looking, he had short black hair and olive, hairless skin. His body was compact and muscular, the body of an athlete, possibly a boxer. This impression was strengthened by his small but flattened broken nose.

The couple looked edgy, glancing off camera as if waiting for some further direction. A voice on the tape broke the silence.

'Remember, Juliet, Paul, I want to see everything.' It was Marcus, out of shot.

Juliet and Paul started to kiss. Paul turned Juliet around to face the camera and he undid her bra, allowing her large breasts to tumble out. The bra fell away and Juliet's purplish nipples stiffened under Paul's eager caress. His fingers then fluttered down her torso and darted beneath the waistband of her knickers. Delight at what he found there spread across his face and Juliet eased out of her pants to reveal his fingers embedded to the knuckle in her hungry sex. Throwing back her head Juliet shimmied her hips, making her breasts sway from side to side.

'Juliet, sit on his thighs, facing me, with your legs open.'

Both Juliet and Paul laughed. 'Anything for you, dear Marcus,' said Juliet and she blew a kiss at the camera.

They did as they were told and the camera moved in, exciting Sam with a close-up of Juliet's labia. Her lips were darker than her nipples and swollen in excited anticipation. Juliet gyrated her hips closer to the camera and Sam could clearly see her clitoris unsheathed and erect. Paul moved his fingers back to her vagina, parting the lips with his index and forefinger and affording the camera a view of Juliet's glistening vulva. It was obvious that she was aroused by being watched and Sam shifted in her armchair, unsettled but fascinated by what was happening on the large TV screen before her.

Paul fingered her for a while and then sucked her juices from his hand. Sam could hear Marcus breathing deeply off screen.

'Let's show Marcus another view of you,' said Paul, lifting Juliet up off his lap.

Juliet turned and knelt on the bed and Paul eased her forwards so that her arms were outstretched on the sheets for balance. He crouched beside her, forcing her legs apart with his knee, and the camera focused on her parted cheeks. Paul spat on his fingers and played around the rim of her anus. The tip of his finger edged just inside and Sam could see the skin puckering at the edges of the tight-looking hole. Juliet moaned but Sam couldn't figure out if this was from pleasure or pain. He left his finger there while his other hand again parted her lips. Juliet was now totally exposed to the camera.

Sam heard herself moaning along with Juliet. She had seen porn tapes before but they had always left her cold. They seemed so artificial and ugly. This one was different. She felt she was being allowed to witness a very intimate moment, the nervousness of the performers only adding to the realism.

Feeling aroused, she unfastened her skirt and placed her hand between her legs, squeezing it with her thighs, feeling the dampness of her lace underwear. Soon her pants joined her skirt on the floor and lying across her sofa, she spread her legs like Juliet's on the TV. She teased herself for a while, fondling her lips, pulling on her pubic hair, dipping her long fingers in and out of herself.

On screen, Paul had taken off his underwear. His short but thick circumcised penis was standing to attention, a shade darker than his tanned body, and he anointed its shiny head with Juliet's love juices. Playing to the camera, he tantalisingly massaged his scrotum, rolling his balls between his wet fingers. Sam imagined herself as Marcus filming this scene and the power she would feel having these two people respond to her desires. She began massaging her clitoris and from the noises off-screen, it sounded as if Marcus had begun to masturbate too.

'Start fucking her.' Marcus's voice broke with the effort of trying to keep his desire under control.

As Paul helped Juliet up on to the bed, the fantasy in Sam's head switched from being the watcher to being watched. She imagined how it would feel to be like Juliet now, lying on her back, legs wide apart, a camera capturing her every secret place in close-up. She wanted to be Juliet, laid bare and vulnerable to Marcus's eyes, watching him in his excitement, watching him masturbate. Sam wanted to be the centre of his desire.

For a moment, the action on the screen seemed to freeze as Marcus's camera zoomed in close on Juliet's well-lubricated sex. For Sam, it was as if her own body was up there on the screen, exposed, contracting, needing to be filled, and her hand began moving faster between her legs. The view on the TV then went fuzzy and the camera pulled back to show that Paul had taken his place between Juliet's thighs.

From the camera angle, Sam could tell that Marcus was now on his knees at the foot of the bed. Juliet had wrapped her legs around Paul's waist, her face now obscured from view. The camera fixed on Paul's taut buttocks, rising to reveal his balls up tight against his body, then falling as he drove his penis deep into Juliet, the width of it making her gasp. Sam's fingers matched his rhythm, imagining the pleasure that he was giving to Juliet, imagining Marcus stroking his own cock as he filmed them, imagining Marcus watching her now, watching this.

Harder and faster she worked her hand, the groans from three people egging on her own. Throwing her head back, she began to cry out as her orgasm enveloped her. Spasm after spasm of pleasure erupted from her very centre and rippled through her stomach, racing up to her breasts. Her whole body shook as Juliet came, noisily, followed quickly by Paul. As the sensations from Sam's vagina began to subside, Marcus let out a long, low moan and the screen went blank.

For several minutes Sam just lay there, shocked by the feelings that had overtaken her, shocked at how much Marcus's proposition excited her and surprised that she hadn't thought once about Toby. Could she do it? She trembled at the thought, then before she knew it her fingers were working their magic again. Stopping herself she jumped up and reached for the phone, her legs weak from the exertion.

She dialled and waited for what seemed like ages, now unsure again of what she was doing. She thought about putting the phone down but it was too late.

'Hello?'

'Marcus, it's Sam.' I can't do it, she thought.

'You sound out of breath.' Sam could hear the amusement in his voice.

'As you may have guessed, I've been watching your little film. Let's just say it was very entertaining.'

Marcus laughed. 'So are you interested?'

There was silence. Sam thought about the list on the fridge: ten years' worth of fantasies. Marcus was offering all of them to her on a plate. She'd be a fool to say no, but she was scared. She wasn't even sure she was up to it.

Marcus's voice interrupted her thoughts, 'Come on, Sam, it's a dream come true.'

'Yes, it could be,' she said and then, in a small voice, 'I'm in.'

'Good.' The phone clicked. Marcus had hung up. Still unsteady, she walked into the kitchen and took the list she had made with Toby off her refrigerator door, and, without looking at it, screwed it up and threw it into the bin.

Sam and Judy were sitting opposite each other at their old haunt, a tiny Mexican restaurant near the office. Cheap and cheerful, the place was far too down-market for their expense account colleagues and they often came here, safe in the knowledge that the subject of their gossip would be unlikely to be sitting at the next table, entertaining a client.

'You know, you never did tell me what happened between you and Marcus,' said Sam.

Her friend laughed. 'It's too embarrassing.'

'Tell me or I'll never let you pay for lunch again.'

'At least let me have a drink first,' replied Judy, helping herself to the pitcher of Sangria. 'Here's to the future.'

'To the future,' said Sam, lifting her glass. 'Which is why I want to know all about you and Marcus.'

Judy took a while to respond. 'There's not that much to tell really. Marcus took me out for dinner when I first started and I slept with him afterwards. I don't really remember much about it. But at least I made it to a bed, unlike Carol Church. You won't remember her, she was fired before you started. Anyway, a few years ago, just before the Christmas party, Hector Rathbone dumped hundreds of spreadsheets on Carol's desk and told her she couldn't go to the party until she'd photocopied every one of them . . .'

Judy's voice faded in Sam's ears as she imagined the small, hot, windowless room. On more than one occasion when she'd been working late with Toby, they had locked themselves in there for a frenzied bout of love-making. Carol, who Sam imagined looked very much like herself, was standing by the photocopier, looking bored as the machine spewed out sheet after sheet of paper.

For the party she was wearing an outrageously expensive dress, fashioned out of the sheerest velvet which had the effect of making her look even taller and slimmer whilst giving a firm outline to her breasts. Bra-less so as not to ruin the line of her outfit, the woman's nipples stood erect under the delicate material. The dress flared out over her hips and stopped mid-thigh, covering her silk cami-knickers and the tops of her seamed suspender-less stockings. She had topped off the outfit with black patent leather stilettos which added four inches to her height. The shoes were made for sex, not comfort.

Silently, Marcus came into the photocopying room and stood behind her. He brushed her long hair to the side and started to kiss the nape of her neck, moving very slowly up to her ear, sending shivers down the woman's spine.

She turned to face him and, for once, he looked ruffled. His tie was undone, as was his shirt collar, and she even thought she could detect a five o'clock shadow. She had to admit she liked this slightly more rugged look. Marcus put his hand in the small of her back and embraced her. At first he kissed her chastely, his lips closed, but then he started to probe her mouth hard with his tongue and she could taste the champagne on his breath. Her lips parted more and she responded to his kisses with the same passion. She wanted him inside her, opening her up.

Her shoes made them the same height and as they stood crotch to groin, she could feel his erection pushing against her. She let one hand slide from around his neck and ran her fingers down his chest, poking in between the buttons on his shirt, then moving down over his belt. She felt the light wool of his trousers tented over the hardness underneath, a hardness which was all for her. He sighed and shifted forward as she traced the outline of his erection. As she began to undo his zip, he stopped her hand and gently broke away.

'We haven't got any time,' said Marcus, his voice full of frustration. 'There's a car waiting outside and any minute now my secretary is going to come looking for me.'

'Then be quick,' she replied.

It took Marcus a second to make a decision. He

twirled the woman around and forced her over the photocopier. He lifted up her dress with one hand while undoing his belt and zip with the other. Then he took off her knickers, admiring the creamy, taut skin of her buttocks. But there was no time for further admiration and releasing his penis, he felt between the woman's legs. Aroused, she rubbed herself against his hand, feeling her lips part across his fingers. She was so wet, she knew that Marcus would be able just to slide right into her. Marcus took his hand away and, grabbing her hips, he lifted her slightly and without further ado, drove his cock straight into her.

She gasped as he entered her with one thrust. Although wet, her vagina had had no preparation for the largeness of him. Being sprawled over the photocopier she couldn't see his face but she could imagine the look of lust in his eyes. Marcus pounded deeper into her and as his penis slammed against her insides she felt a delicious pain. She just wanted him to fuck her as hard and as quick as he could, to use her for his pleasure.

Marcus was moving faster and faster as he neared orgasm, slamming his hips against her bottom. He grabbed her hair and yanked her head back as he started to come. Inside her she could feel his cock pulsate as spurt after spurt of semen entered her. She reached down to satiate her tormented clitoris while Marcus, losing none of his hardness, continued to pound her slick vagina. But seconds away from her orgasm, they were interrupted by a knock on the door.

'Mr McLeod, are you in there? It's nine o'clock.'

Marcus quickly withdrew. 'I'll be right there,

Phyllis,' he said stuffing his hard cock back into his trousers. He glanced back at Carol. 'I'm sorry, but I've got another appointment.'

He unlocked the door and disappeared, leaving Carol still bent over the photocopier, his come dribbling down her thighs.

'Poor Carol,' said Judy. 'She said that she would have given up her Christmas bonus if he'd just finished the job.'

Sam seemed miles away, absent-mindedly crumbling tortillas between her fingers.

'She got the sack when people saw the photocopies. Sam, are you listening to me?'

Sam blushed. 'Of course I am. What, she really got the sack for that?'

'No, she was an appalling typist. Anyway, that's how Marcus is, the love 'em and leave 'em type.'

'Did he finish off the job with you?'

'I'm ashamed to admit I can hardly remember. I was completely paralytic. Anyway, what's Marcus offering you?'

To conceal her embarrassment, Sam waved at a waitress and pointed to the empty pitcher in front of her. 'I'm not sure yet but you know what a disaster our relationship was before.'

'Is it once bitten, twice shy?' quizzed Judy.

'I'm no fool.'

'I know that. All I'm saying is just be careful.'

'I will. So who's sleeping with who at WR this week?'

The rest of the evening was spent laughing about past and present foibles of the company's employees. There was an edge of sadness for Sam that she was no longer part of these other people's lives.

Paying the bill, Judy asked Sam about her immediate plans.

'I want to look at some old newspaper cuttings. I need to check out the insider dealing stuff on Marcus.'

'Good luck to you. That man plays everything close to his chest.'

Outside the restaurant, the two women hugged.

'I'll ring you tomorrow, Sherlock,' said Judy, kissing Sam on the cheek and leaving just a smudge of her lipstick.

Once back in her flat, Sam turned on her CD player. The music soothed her and made her feel a little less lonely. Pouring herself a gin and tonic, she settled down to read her file marked 'McLeod'.

As she looked through the cuttings she noted that many seemed to use the insider dealing accusation only as a peg to delve into Marcus's private life. There were dozens of photographs of him with a variety of beautiful women draped on his arm. Including her. She came across the photograph of herself looking dazed and confused outside her flat. Despite diligently cutting out all the articles on Marcus, she'd been too upset to read anything about him at the time, but now she felt completely removed from the frightened young girl in the picture. It was fascinating to see part of her life played out in the Press.

Reading through the articles, Sam was relieved to find that the writers had been fairly kind about her involvement with Marcus. Unfortunately, they were less charitable towards him. There was much innuendo about his sexual prowess and long lists had been compiled of the well-known women he'd supposedly bedded. It riled her the way the journalists hypocritically denounced his activities while at the same writing about them in lurid detail. A few of the women writers begrudgingly admitted to his attractiveness but when it came to their male colleagues, all the knives were out. The snobbery around his humble beginnings was incredible, the general tone being, well, what can you expect of somebody with his background?

The actual details on the insider dealing were vague. The basic argument seemed to be that Marcus had bought shares in a company called Northern TV whilst dating Harriet Bowman, the Chairman's daughter, and so therefore, must have known about its imminent takeover. The investigation by the Department of Trade and Industry had found no evidence to bring a prosecution. This wasn't any consolation to Sam. She'd been around the City long enough to realise that many still saw white-collar crime as victimless; prosecutions against big City names were few and far between. The DTI might have exonerated him but it didn't mean Marcus was innocent.

It was getting late and Sam decided to call it a night. Mr McLeod could wait.

Marcus had called Sam to a nine a.m. meeting at his offices in Gracechurch Street. From the number of cigarette butts in the ashtray on his desk, Sam could tell he'd already been working for a couple of hours.

Marcus sat back in his chair and smiled at her.

'Good morning, Sam. Are you ready for our first wager?'

'As ready as I'll ever be.' In the cold light of day, Marcus's offer seemed very clinical. She was apprehensive about the way she'd deal with him if she lost the bet.

'We'll start with something easy,' said Marcus, looking completely untroubled by the bizarre nature of their arrangement. 'You've got a very good chance of winning. What I want you to do is look at the top twenty Blue Chip companies and tell me which one you think is going to be taken over in the next week.'

'That seems a bit too easy. I take it there's a catch?'

'Not at all, Sam. You have so little faith in me,' he said, eyes wide with mock hurt.

'Too right,' she said, goading him on.

'The odds are two to one. How much will you be betting?'

Sam knew that if she said a hundred pounds he'd laugh her out of the office. She took a big breath. 'Five thousand.'

'Fine.'

She excused herself and spent the rest of the day in the Business Library sifting through laborious business reports and reading the latest appraisal of each of the twenty companies. She desperately wanted to beat Marcus, to prove she was better than him, to see his face as she took ten thousand pounds off him and to hear the disappointment in his voice when he knew there was no forfeit to pay.

At about five she called him from the pay phone outside the library.

'So who are you betting on?' he asked.

'I'm not sure if any are going to be taken over. What are the rules if nothing happens?'

'The bet is null and void and you get to keep the five thousand.'

'Great,' replied Sam. This was going to be easy money. She was pretty sure from all that she had read that there was no takeover activity happening. 'But if I have to choose one, I'll go for MacPherson's. The pharmaceuticals market is fairly volatile, don't you think?'

'It doesn't matter what I think. But my money's on Brady's and I've got seven days starting from tomorrow to prove I'm right.'

Sam hung up, unnerved by his confidence.

She didn't have to wait a week. Only two days later, she stood in her hallway flicking through the just-delivered *Financial Times*. Rooted to the spot, she read the headline on the friendly takeover of Brady's. All signed and delivered the night before. She hadn't even made it to the living room when the telephone started ringing.

'The forfeit's tonight,' was Marcus's opening address.

'You knew about it all the time, didn't you?'

'Ask me no questions . . .' came his maddening reply.

Sam said nothing.

'Come on, Sam, you aren't really losing, are you?'

She took a second to think about it. The challenge of beating Marcus at his own game had been the central focus for her. She had forgotten the other side of the bargain and if the truth were known she wanted that as much winning. 'I guess you're right,' she begrudgingly replied.

45

'A car will pick you up at eight tonight.'

The drive to the Mayfair apartment was excruciating. Marcus had given her instructions on what to wear. Or rather, what not to wear. And so she sat in the back of his limousine wearing only a basque and stockings beneath her mac; Marcus had forbidden the wearing of knickers. Beset with nerves, Sam squirmed throughout the whole journey wondering how much the driver knew about tonight's arrangement. But if the driver knew anything he wasn't letting on and he delivered her to Marcus's door in silence.

Sam rang the bell and was buzzed in by the building's concierge.

'I'm visiting Mr McLeod,' she said brusquely. Again she had the irrational feeling that this man knew what was happening. But all he said was, 'Name?'

'Sam Winterton.'

He looked at a list. 'Take the lift to the penthouse,' he said without even looking up.

In the lift, Sam took the opportunity to examine herself in the mirror. She had piled her black hair high and put on more make-up than usual. If she was going to play the part of a tart she wanted to look it. Then, unexpectedly, her coat fell open, revealing her near naked state underneath. Seeing her own nudity against such an unfamiliar background excited her and, in a moment of pure brazen daring, she slipped out of her coat completely. In for a penny, in for a pound, she told herself as she straightened her stocking, letting one hand graze briefly against her sex and feeling its wetness. The lift came to a juddering halt and the doors opened into a circular hallway.

Summoning up every ounce of nerve, Sam strode into the hallway, trailing her coat on the floor behind her. She called Marcus's name but there was no reply. Her nerve faltered and she wanted badly to put the coat back on. She walked into a room which she had rightly guessed to be the sitting room. Marcus rarely used the apartment and Sam suspected the red-walled room had been prepared not long before her arrival with the dust sheets being taken off the heavy red and gold brocade sofas, the twelve-foot French windows thrown open to the airlessness of the London summer evening and the huge, ornately carved mirror on the far wall lovingly polished.

Suddenly, someone coughed behind her. She whirled around, expecting to see Marcus, but instead she was confronted by a stranger.

'Who the hell are you?' asked Sam, her voice an octave higher than usual, enveloped in shame.

'I'm Steve, a friend of Marcus's. I'm here for the same reason you are,' he said, in a broad London accent.

Sam held her coat to her body. She was confused. Had this Steve lost a bet with Marcus too? Did this mean he was going to sleep with Marcus? And where was Marcus? Then it clicked. She was the one who would be having sex with Steve. She looked at him more closely.

He couldn't have been more than twenty but despite his youth, Sam fancied that she recognised a great similarity to Marcus. He had that same slightly preening arrogance about him, although Sam was certain that at his age he would have much less to be arrogant about. Another twenty years, maybe, she thought. And yet his self-assured demeanour had something. His brown hair was slicked back from a face that couldn't quite be described as handsome, his features too young to have acquired much masculine charm. But his dark, wide-eyed stare revealed his obvious lust and his youthful cockiness excited her.

Her lack of attire should have made her feel vulnerable but she was beginning to enjoy the eroticism of the moment. She could be in control, if she so chose. She knew how to handle a mere boy like this. Unashamedly, her eyes moved down his body. He was dressed in typical City attire, pin-stripe shirt, braces and grey trousers with a slightly too loud red Prince of Wales check. Sam guessed he was a market trader. He was slightly shorter than Sam but broad and he looked as if he'd have no difficulty lifting her up.

After five minutes of sizing each other up, Sam broke the silence. 'Where's Marcus?'

'He's here,' said Steve, looking at the large mirror on the sitting-room wall.

Sam suddenly remembered that once, in an off guard moment, she had told Marcus of her exhibitionistic fantasy of being watched while making love but without being able to see the voyeur. This wasn't quite the scenario she'd envisaged but she could feel the excitement building inside of her.

'Behind there?' she asked, pointing to the mirror.

Steve nodded. Sam took a deep breath and dropped her coat to an appreciative gasp from the mesmerised boy.

'So what happens now?' she asked provocatively.

'I've got my instructions,' said Steve, reasserting his authority, and he led her to one of the overstuffed sofas. In front of it was a large, low, glass-topped coffee table, too modern and out of place with the rest of the room. It seemed to Sam that Marcus had suffered a rare lapse in taste.

Brushing aside this thought she sat facing the mirror. Steve knelt in front of her and spread her legs, immediately giving himself and Marcus a glimpse of her vulva. Obviously not wanting to block Marcus's view he got up and sat next to her and with one hand spread her labia apart. He rotated his index finger around her clitoris so it emerged from its sheath. His experienced manoeuvres belied his youth and Sam squirmed appreciatively. Marcus is watching me, she thought, opening her legs slightly wider.

Sam could feel her juices welling up. The thought that Marcus could clearly see her sex and its response to Steve's hands was almost too much to bear. Steve stopped and moved on to her breasts. He pulled down the cups of the basque so that although her breasts were exposed they were still fully supported by the underwiring, making them look larger than they really were. He bent forward and sucked each nipple in turn, making them hard and erect. Sam wasn't quite sure what was expected of her. She moved her hand to Steve's groin.

'Not yet,' he said, brushing her hand away.

Steve knelt on the sofa and bent forward, placing his head on Sam's stomach, once again fingering her clitoris. Soon his finger was replaced by his tongue and Sam groaned. Now and then Steve would look up at the mirror, almost anxiously, as if he wanted to make sure he was doing the right thing by Marcus. It was clear that Steve was every bit as much in the man's thrall as she was.

Sam knew that in this position Marcus could see everywhere Steve's tongue went. She had no doubt he could see the wetness as it trickled down her inner lips or the way her juices had spread across the boy's eager face. Steve's tongue started to move faster and at the same time he put two fingers into her vagina. His tongue and fingers worked in unison, making Sam moan in delight.

'Harder,' she gasped.

Sam looked straight at the mirror, trying to imagine what Marcus was seeing and what he was doing. Performing like this for Marcus, allowing another man to expose her for his pleasure, was the biggest part of the turn-on. She imagined how wanton she must look, with her breasts propped up and her legs spread far apart as another man used her.

Steve stopped abruptly.

'Don't stop, please, I'm begging you.'

Sam touched herself, feeling the warm wetness. Steve glanced at the mirror, almost as if he were waiting for directions. As she rubbed her clitoris, Steve put his fingers back in, this time using one more. Sam spread her legs even further apart, her vulva so open Marcus couldn't help but see how far up Steve's fingers were going. This thought sent her over the edge and she came. She closed her eyes and was lost in the delight of her own

50

body. Both Sam and Steve were now shouting, 'Yes, yes, yes.'

As her orgasm ebbed away she opened her eyes and was startled to see Marcus in a white towelling bathrobe, now sitting on the sofa opposite. The robe was open and his large penis jutted out in front of him.

'I think I've paid the forfeit, don't you?' said Sam, crossing her legs, feeling uncomfortable now the pleasure had waned.

'We're not finished yet,' said Marcus, taking his penis in his hand. 'I noticed you looking at that table when you came in. It's out of place, isn't it?'

Sam nodded.

'But it has its purpose,' he said, skinning back his foreskin over his swollen glans.

Steve took off his clothes and when he was naked, Sam compared the two men while wondering what they were going to do to her next. Steve's penis, though not as large as Marcus's, stood ramrod stiff, almost pressing against his navel with the urgency of youth. His muscles were more defined than Marcus's, although the comparison of a man in his mid-forties with a twenty-year-old seemed a little unfair. And given the choice, she knew which man she'd like now between her thighs. She looked at Marcus's penis again, transfixed by it, wanting it inside her.

But the choice was not hers to make. She only knew that she would agree to Marcus's pleasure whatever form that took. The two men were exchanging glances, Steve still waiting for Marcus to give his instructions.

'I'd like you to sit on the table, Sam,' said Marcus.

51

She looked at him warily and put her hand on the table as if testing its strength. 'I'm not too sure this is a good idea.'

'On the table. Now.'

Sam sat on the table, feeling its coldness against her labia, her wetness smearing the glass. She knew what would happen next and the knowledge of this brought a fresh warmth to her crotch. As she had predicted to herself, Marcus then slid underneath the table until his face was looking up between her legs. She pressed her sex hard against the glass and Marcus's breathing grew heavy. Steve was watching her intently, now masturbating too.

'Now?' Steve asked.

'Take her!' ordered Marcus.

Sam lay back on the table, still scared that it might not support her weight but wanting so much to do this for Marcus. She spread her legs wide and Steve entered her. He built up a rhythm of short, hard stabs and Sam, still so close to her last orgasm, felt the sensations beginning again. The coffee table creaked under their weight but Sam was past caring. She knew that Marcus was down there watching Steve's assault on her sex and fisting his cock, so aroused because of her. Again her orgasm exploded and she screamed as Steve came too, his face contorted in a snarl of passion. And as her juices, now mixed with Steve's, seeped out of her on to the table top, Marcus's groans reached a crescendo and he came, the white fluid hitting against the underside of the glass.

Chapter Four

THE NEXT DAY Sam finished looking at the McLeod file. She flipped through most of it, knowing that the cuttings weren't going to tell her much more about Marcus. And deep down, Sam knew the truth anyway.

It was only eleven a.m. Sam wondered what to do with herself until the appointment she had made with a stockbroker friend who just might have some work for her. Seeing the photographs of herself in the cuttings gave her the idea of sorting out, once and for all, the shoe box full of photos which she kept under her bed.

Sam knelt on the bedroom floor and hesitantly dragged out the box. She wasn't quite sure if she felt ready to walk down memory lane. There were bound to be plenty of photos of Toby and her. But noticing it was only ten minutes later than when she last looked at a clock, she decided she might just as well fill up her time. Sitting around, doing nothing was anathema to Sam.

She plonked herself on the bed and tipped out the box's contents. The first picture she picked up was of Judy and her on a skiing holiday in France, several years before. She noted that, although she was smiling at the camera, she didn't look as assured then as she did today, despite losing Toby and her job. She now felt an inner confidence that seemed absent in the photo, which showed her with her shoulders hunched and her hair purposely styled forward to shield her face.

The next photo made Sam laugh out loud. It was a picture a boyfriend called Ray had taken of her when they were in the sixth form together. At the time she probably would never have believed that the girl who took evening classes in Marxist economics and had a Che Guevara poster on the wall would end up becoming a capitalist stockbroker. Although from the photo there was some indication of her sexual adventurousness.

Sam remembered how Ray had told her that he had a thing about secretaries. She had dressed accordingly but it had transpired that Ray preferred his secretaries in a state of undress. And here was the proof. Sam was sitting in front of a typewriter, dressed only in bra, knickers and black stilettos. Her hair was styled in a bun as Ray had told her this was how the secretaries of his fantasies always looked. Sam had painted her lips a deep red and was giving the camera a come hither smile. She briefly wondered what happened to Ray. The last Sam had heard he'd got married and had two kids.

The next photograph completely wiped the smile off her face. If a picture speaks a thousand words this one told the story of the beginning of Sam's transition into a career woman who would never again be beholden to a man. Julian O'Connor, what a bastard, she thought. Even now, six years later, the very thought of him made her hackles rise. He was the reason she wouldn't go to Japan with Toby.

Sam had been with Julian six months when he had a job offer from America. He had begged Sam to go with him, telling her that it would be a great new start, that they'd explore and conquer the States together. Thinking she was in love, Sam readily agreed. But the reality of living in their high-rent, small-roomed apartment in an unfashionable part of New York was something else.

When Julian wasn't working he was out boozing with his new buddies, not caring that Sam, who couldn't get a Green Card and therefore couldn't work, was going out of her mind with boredom. She knew nobody in New York then. On the few occasions when Julian was at home, he treated her like the little wifey, expecting her to spend her days coming up with fabulous new recipes to cook for him and entertain him with tales about the wonderful new cleaning products she'd tried.

When she told him how she felt he called her ungrateful and told her to fuck off back to Britain. Sam didn't need to be told twice. The experience knocked her for six, and after that her affairs with men were kept pretty low key until Marcus came along. She had felt ready to trust Marcus and once again she'd been disappointed, although she now accepted that he never intended to hurt her. When Toby appeared in her life she found herself, almost against her will, opening up, little by little. But not quite enough that she would go abroad with him without her own job and independence.

Sam spread the photos across the bed to find a picture of Toby. The one she picked up had been taken only a month or so before he left. They had gone to Brighton for a romantic weekend. Typically, it had rained and blown a gale as they tried to walk along the promenade but it hadn't mattered. Sam remembered how warm she had felt inside, cared for and cherished. Neither had known about Toby's new job then.

They had gone to a sex shop and giggled like school children as they studied a variety of sex toys. Toby had gallantly bought Sam a six-inch vibrator *and* a twelve-inch dildo for the nights that he might not be with her. Did he have a premonition then that she would have many nights without him?

Another picture from that weekend was taken by a professional photographer in a restaurant. Sam felt the tears well up. They made a perfect couple, as many friends had told them at the time. *C'est la vie*, thought Sam bitterly as she gathered up all the photographs. She was no nearer sorting them out but now she didn't have the heart to do it. She tried to console herself that in a couple of years she could look at the photos of Toby and her and feel nothing at all. A small voice in her said 'some hope'.

Well, at least looking at the photographs had passed the time. She knew she should get ready for her meeting with Martin Spencer. His firm, Spencer & Co., was very small time in the world of stockbroking but beggars couldn't be choosers, and she still wasn't sure about Marcus and his idea of helping her. Also, she wanted to ask Martin's advice on her own personal share dealings, as the state of her finances was dire.

She showered and dressed in her favourite grey suit. With its long jacket and short skirt, its perfect cut advertised the phenomenal price it had cost her. She applied only a smidgen of pale pink lipstick and mascara and put her hair up in a topknot before deciding that it looked better down.

'Come in, come in,' ushered Martin, holding the door open for Sam. 'How are you?'

'Fine.'

She followed behind him, noting the rabbit warren of tiny offices with only the odd dying cheese plant as a sign that there was a world of nature outside the all-consuming realm of finance with its computer terminals, faxes and mobile phones. She wasn't sure if she could work in this set-up even if there was a job going.

Before she could mention her doubts, Martin pre-empted her. 'I think you've had a wasted journey down here, Sam.'

'Oh,' said Sam, trying to keep the hopefulness out of her voice.

'I've looked hard at what we can actually offer you, the only thing we could give you at an equivalent level to what you were doing at Walker, Rathbone, is some temporary work. Anything else would be junior stuff. I wouldn't like to insult your intelligence by offering you that.'

'It's all right, Martin, I've got a few other things

in the pipeline. I'm sure I'll be fine,' said Sam, with more confidence than she felt. 'But,' she continued, 'while I'm here, perhaps you could give me some advice on some personal share transactions.'

He seemed relieved that he could help Sam in some way. She wondered if what Judy had heard was true, that Martin was infatuated with Sam. As nice as he was, he just wasn't her type: too short and thin for her liking. Also, when he was around Sam, he tended to look like a rabbit caught in a car's headlights. She could eat him for breakfast.

They spent the next half hour comfortably speculating over what shares Sam should buy and sell. She needed to make money. There was to be no flamboyant gambling with her cash as she had done with clients. Sam felt satisfied that her hunches were correct and started to pack up.

'Thanks ever so much for your time, Martin.'

'Any time,' he said, with a huge grin across his face. 'Have you ever thought about investing in agriculture?' he added out of the blue.

'Too volatile, Martin, you know that.'

He nodded. 'Just an idea.'

Sam told him not to bother seeing her to the door and promised to speak to him in the near future.

She made her way through the crowded street. It was night-time, but light coming from the huge neon signs on the buildings which lined the narrow street made it as bright as day. Occasionally she would stop somebody and show them a picture of Toby, asking if they'd seen him, but nobody seemed to understand what she was saying. She grew panicky. The force of the crowd against her grew stronger, heavier, lifting her up off her feet. She fell to the ground in a forest of legs and the picture of Toby slipped from her grasp and was carried away.

She awoke with a start. Half asleep, it took her a few seconds to realise that the sound which had roused her was a knock on the door. Sam looked at her alarm clock. It was only eight a.m. Who the hell was at her door at this time? The knocking continued.

'Okay, okay,' she shouted, quickly throwing on her dressing gown. 'Give me a minute.'

She opened the door to find a young delivery boy. At his feet was a small leather-bound chest, padlocked, with a key attached to a note on the lid.

'Ms Winterton?'

'Yes?'

'The doorman told me to come on up. It's from Mr McLeod. Sign here, please.'

Not yet fully awake, Sam took several seconds to respond, trying to remember what she had agreed to do for Marcus. The nonchalance of the delivery boy suggested that he had no knowledge of the chest's contents.

She signed the docket and dragged the chest into her living room. Her hands shook with apprehension as she ripped open the envelope. Inside was a note in elegant copperplate handwriting which read:

Sam, As you will probably now know, the livestock prices on which you gambled actually went down. I should blame the EC and those animal-rights groups if I were you. Nevertheless I win again and the terms of our

59

arrangement mean you're about to embark on another forfeit. I think the punishment should fit the crime, don't you?

Instead of Marcus's signature there was a red wax seal bearing the imprint of his signet ring.

Sam held the key in her hand for a while, wondering how the contents of the chest would be a fit punishment for her supposed crime. Livestock prices? The obvious answer was too horrible to contemplate. Gingerly, she undid the padlock and lifted the lid of the chest. Inside were several objects wrapped in purple tissue paper.

She unwrapped the first to reveal a pair of long black gloves made from the softest calfskin. Leather wear! She laughed at having jumped to such a ridiculous conclusion about the nature of her forfeit. She held the gloves to her face and breathed in the intoxicating aroma of new leather.

She took off her dressing gown and slipped on the gloves, excited by the thought of what there might be yet to come in the chest. The gloves quickly grew warm from her body heat and she delighted in the way that the leather softly clung to her arms. From its shape she guessed that the next parcel in the chest would contain boots. But she hadn't guessed how high they were: unwrapping them, she found that the legs had been folded in half. They were thigh-length, with what looked like a six-inch heel, and were done up with laces at the side. They were also made of black leather, although of a much sturdier kind than the gloves.

Slowly, savouring the experience, Sam put on the boots and tied the laces tight against her thighs. She stood up, a little shaky on the heels.

She now stood over six feet tall and she had to admit to herself that the boots gave her a feeling of power.

There were two parcels left and she opened the larger of the two. Marcus had sent her a leather harness. Made up of numerous belts, buckles and studs, the harness had leather plates to cover her breasts with detachable sections to reveal her nipples. Attached to the waist belt of the harness was a similarly removable leather G-string. Sam decided to unwrap the final parcel before trying on the harness. In it was a leather-bound copy of *120 Days of Sodom* by de Sade. Sam opened the book and a card fell on to the floor.

She put the book to one side and retrieved the card, which was an advert for a club happening on Friday night. On it was a picture of a woman dressed in an outfit similar to hers. The woman was on her knees, gagged and blindfolded. A bare-chested man dressed in riding boots and leather trousers stood above her menacingly. The club was called Pain.

Sam closed the lid of the chest and sat on it wondering what to do next. She didn't want the book – she'd read it as a rebellious teenager and had found it quite dull. She wasn't into pain. She couldn't think what satisfaction Marcus would derive from seeing her hurt. She picked up the harness and went into her bedroom with the idea of phoning Marcus to tell him that she was going to renege on the deal. Then she caught sight of herself in the mirror and stopped.

She loved the way the black of the leather contrasted with the whiteness of her skin. She ran her hands over her body, enjoying the touch of this animal skin against her own soft flesh. Looking at the harness again Sam decided to try it on. It was quite complicated working out which bit went where, but once on the effect was stunning. Her breast showed slightly on each side of the leather bra. As she turned around to look at herself from behind she noted how the belt, which fitted between her legs, accentuated her firm buttocks, giving a line which invited one to touch wherever it led. She then attached the G-string. She felt like an Amazon, ready to do battle. But at Pain would she be dominatrix or dominated?

Whichever way it went, she knew that being dressed up in this manner excited her. She undid the breast pads and slowly played with her pink nipples which poked out from underneath, picturing Marcus doing the same to her. The effect of imagining him in front of her, licking her breasts, made her wet and she could feel the slight chafing of the leather thong against her labia.

Aroused, she decided she couldn't wait until Friday to be satisfied; she wanted to respond to the effect the leather had now. Crossing the room, she opened the drawer in her bedside cabinet and, amongst her arsenal of sex toys, she found the vibrator Toby had bought for her in Brighton. Returning to the mirror she sat on the edge of the bed with her legs stretched wide open.

The thong was strapped tight against her vagina, allowing her to see a vague outline of her lips and pubis. At first, she just gently massaged herself over the top of the leather but as her excitement increased she began to press harder.

62

Would this be what Marcus would do? The thought of his firm hands touching the most intimate part of her made her even wetter. She knew she could only tease herself for a few minutes more. Her vagina ached and only an orgasm would bring her relief.

She undid the thong's ties and the triangular piece of leather came away in her hand. She threw it to one side and spent some moments watching the effect of having only the harness's groin strap to hide herself. It neatly did what it was meant to do and divided her labia. She gently stroked her lips, then, not wanting to waste any more time, she unclipped the strap so her vulva was free.

At first, she used just her fingers to stroke her clitoris but the need to come became so strong she turned on her vibrator. Lifting her legs slightly, she pushed the vibrator inside herself. The vibrations gently shook her whole body. She pushed it in and out a few times, watching it disappear. Then she slowly withdrew it, and, having lubricated it with her moisture, it slid easily up between her lips to her clitoris.

The vibrations made the blood rush into her clit. She had no time for fantasising as she came almost immediately. She left the vibrator on her clitoris and seconds later she was having a second orgasm. She moaned out loud and squeezed her thighs together, wringing out the last drop of her orgasm. She lay back on the bed, her heart thumping. It occurred to her that although men ruled the world they couldn't have multiple orgasms, and that was surely some compensation. She was tempted to start again but decided that she would force herself to wait two more days until Friday.

A taxi drove her to Pain and once again she wore only her mac to cover her unusual outfit. As they arrived at the club, Sam blushed. There was a queue of people ouside the door and unlike her, very few of them had tried to hide what they were wearing. She tried to ignore the taxi driver's sneer as she paid him. She was unsure what to do next. Deciding to be bold, she walked to the front of the queue and mentioned Marcus's name to the doorman. She was immediately shown into the club.

The place was dimly lit with red lights and the walls appeared to be black. Sam could hear the thump of what sounded like tribal drumming. Television screens hung from the ceilings showing videos of people being tattooed on the most intimate areas of their bodies. The whole atmosphere of the place made her nervous.

Adjusting her eyes to the dim light, Sam looked around at the club's other guests. She had felt very daring when getting ready for her date but now, looking around, she felt almost tame in comparison to some of the others. In front of her was a woman wearing a basque with only a quarter-cup bra which revealed her heavily pierced nipples. As startling as this was, it wasn't this that stunned Sam. For in her hand the woman held a leather dog lead which was attached to her partner by a piercing which went through the head of his exposed penis. To Sam's amazement, he didn't even flinch as she tugged at him to move on.

To the right of her stood a woman dressed in a leather bra with matching pants. Protruding from the front of the pants was an imitation penis. The attire of her partner seemed more conservative – just a pair of leather trousers. However, when he turned around, Sam noticed that the leather trousers were, in fact, chaps like the ones cowboys wore in films over their jeans. But the man was wearing nothing underneath and was showing off a very pert butt.

'Can I take your coat?' A man dressed in leather shorts and cap was holding out his hand. He continued, 'Marcus is upstairs waiting for you. The fourth floor.'

Did everyone know Marcus? she wondered. Maybe he had staged the whole event for her. She almost wished he had – what a compliment that would be. Her every sexual wish, his command. She took off her coat and, for a second, felt like putting it on again as the man in shorts gave her an appraising look. But she realised she was being silly – you didn't dress up like this for people not to look at you.

The man pointed to the stairs for the fourth floor. Sam thanked him and made her way through sweating bodies which were dressed or rather undressed in a similar fashion to the people she had already seen. She wondered what was on the other floors but realised she was already late and kept on going.

As she neared the fourth floor she could hear an odd cracking noise. It took her some time to work out what it was. Then she twigged. It was the sound of leather meeting flesh. She stopped. Surely, Marcus hadn't planned for her to be whipped? Why would he do this to her? He'd promised that this arrangement would be mutually beneficial. She couldn't imagine enjoying being whipped. Once or twice she had thought of Toby bending her over and caning her but she wasn't at all sure she could manage the pain.

She took a deep breath as she entered the room. It was darker here than it had been downstairs. In the dimness, she made out that all around the room were X-shaped wooden crosses, with a person tied to each. She saw that there were just as many men tied to the crosses as women. On one, a woman in a red lace basque and stockings was being caned on her bare buttocks by a woman in a similar outfit. The woman with the cane had the most constricted waist Sam had ever seen.

'More, please, mistress,' begged the tied woman.

Her mistress kindly acquiesced. Sam noticed the red welts on the slave's behind and shuddered.

She peered around the room for Marcus but couldn't see him. Instead, her eyes alighted on a man in a similar harness to her own bent over a school horse. He, too, was being severely punished by his mistress who was brandishing what looked like a leather paddle. Sam decided she was going to leave but as she turned to go she bumped into Marcus.

'What fetish is that?' she asked him, noticing the fact that unlike everybody else in the club, Marcus was casually dressed in a polo neck and jeans.

He laughed. 'We're not here for me, are we, Sam?'

Before she could tell him that she wasn't prepared to submit to any torture, Marcus revealed that he had a riding crop behind his back. He gently stroked her bottom with the tasselled end of it and then lightly tapped her crotch. Despite her fears, Sam could feel the damp warmth where he was tapping. Marcus drew the outline of her lips with the tip of the crop and Sam moved her body against him, aware of his growing excitement. Instead of continuing, Marcus threw the crop on the floor and said, 'Come and see the rest of the club.'

He took her down one flight of stairs and into another dark room. In a corner, a line of people stood waiting to go into a smaller room, divided off from the main area by a curtain. Marcus led Sam to the front of the queue and winked knowingly at the man who drew the curtain aside for them to enter.

Inside there were about ten people looking through peepholes made in an imitation brick wall. Sam's curiosity was aroused and she quickly found a hole to look through. The hole was barely four feet from the ground and she had to bend over to see properly. She gasped at the sight in front of her. Lying on a bed covered in blue velvet was a dark-haired woman in her early thirties, dressed only in a red bra, stockings and suspenders, masturbating herself for the audience's pleasure. Sam could hear others in the room moaning with delight at the sight.

Sam was fascinated. She had never seen, in real life, a woman playing with herself. The woman made sure that everyone could savour the sight. She slowly pushed her fingers in and out of her vagina. It was obvious that she was excited. Taking her fingers out, she leaned over the bed and found a large black dildo. She tantalised the audience by placing the head at the entrance of her sex.

Marcus was not watching the display. He stood behind Sam and massaged her bare buttocks, occasionally going very close to her vagina. But not close enough. Sam wriggled and closed her legs together tightly. She felt torn between carrying on watching to find out what the woman would do with the dildo next and turning her attention to Marcus to beg him to touch her like the dildo was touching the woman. She chose to continue watching, hoping Marcus would sense her need.

The audience had started to shout in unison, telling the woman what they wanted her to do next. She obliged them and rammed the dildo all the way up inside herself. Sam could see how it stretched the woman open, the way her lips closed around the sides of the tool and made the woman's clitoris bulge even more prominently. As the woman began fucking herself with the dildo, using one hand to rub her clitoris, it became clear that she was no longer playing to the crowd. This was now all for her own pleasure.

Sam touched herself with her own fingers, hoping that Marcus might take over. But he didn't and Sam kept playing with herself, sliding her fingers under the thong to touch the soft, wet flesh. The woman moaned faster and louder until she reached a crescendo signifying her orgasm.

The audience clapped appreciatively and the woman made a slight bow with her head, smiling lasciviously.

Sam was disappointed that it had ended and that she herself hadn't come. She looked at Marcus but his thoughts and feelings were unfathomable. He took her arm and escorted her out of the room and down to the next floor. Perhaps here he would satisfy her. Her frustration was becoming unbearable.

The next room was much lighter than the rest of the club. White, billowing nets fell from the ceiling and the centre of the room was covered in scatter cushions, although Sam could hardly see the cushions for the writhing mass of bodies on top of them. She looked on in amazement at the daisy-chain sex taking place. One man would be performing cunnilingus on a woman who would be fellating another man who, in turn, would be fingering another woman. Another group had a woman on all fours being fucked from behind while a woman lay underneath her breasts, sucking noisily on her nipples. Sam turned to Marcus.

'Are we going to join in?'

'Oh no, I have different plans for you upstairs. I just thought you'd enjoy this little spectacle.'

Sam admitted she did and then asked, 'What's going to happen upstairs?'

'Wait and see,' came the reply.

They returned to the room with the crosses. Different people were now tied to them with different mistresses and masters. Sam grabbed Marcus's hand.

'You're not going to tie me to a cross, are you?'

'Patience, patience,' replied Marcus, gently nudging her towards the corner of the room.

There a door opened and out came a man who towered above Sam. His body was lightly oiled, showing off his muscular physique to its best effect. He was dressed in a leather harness and chaps and on his head he wore a leather mask which had holes for his eyes, nose and mouth. He stood silently with his legs apart, his big semi-erect penis dangling freely between his legs. Sam just stared at him. His arms and chest were covered in beautiful tattoos of eagles and tigers. She noticed that both his nipples were pierced with large brass rings. In his right hand, he held a leather whip which had a handle shaped like a phallus.

Sam was near speechless as she imagined being tied to the cross while this man whipped her and then penetrated her with the whip handle.

'No, Marcus,' she finally said.

Marcus came and stood right behind her, lightly stroking her rear. 'Sam, he's your slave. Do what you like with him.'

A ripple of pleasure rolled through her body and she smiled – she would be the one in charge and this man who was twice her size would be under her command. She signalled to him to come over to her. Trying out her new authority, she told him to kneel. He did as he was told.

'Lick me,' she ordered.

The man knew exactly what she wanted. He licked the leather of her G-string and Sam could feel the pressure of his tongue.

'Closer,' she whispered.

His tongue poked under the G-string and

touched her lips. The man then looked up at her. 'May I take this off, mistress?' he asked, pointing to the piece of leather that was preventing him from going to work on her.

'Yes,' came Sam's clipped reply.

Once it was off he elbowed her legs slightly apart and started to lick up and down her swollen lips. Both mistress and slave were frustrated by the crotch strap still preventing him licking her and entering her with his tongue. Sam impatiently unclipped it and the man appeared to breathe a sigh of relief as his tongue slid effortlessly into her wet hole.

So caught up in her pleasures, Sam didn't at first notice that a group of people had gathered to watch the spectacle. Being surrounded by so many people worried her and she scanned the crowd to find Marcus. He was standing in the shadows with an encouraging smile on his face, and reassured by his presence, Sam returned her attention to the delicious sensations happening between her legs. Relaxing into it, she realised that she was thrilled to be the focus of so many people's desire and this realisation made her bold.

She knew that the slave would have been content to stay lapping between her thighs for as long as she ordered, but she had other plans for him. She slapped his head away from her crotch and ordered him to stand up. She took the dildo-whip from his hand and ran the handle between the crack of his exposed buttocks. The murmurs from the crowd grew louder, encouraging Sam to penetrate her slave, abuse him. Unexpectedly, she lifted the whip in the air and cracked it.

'Shut up!' she ordered the onlookers.

She was the dominatrix and she would do whatever she pleased.

The crowd was silent, bowing to Sam's control. She led her slave to one of the crosses and chained his wrists and ankles to the wooden beams so that he was spread-eagled. His now fully engorged cock stabbed at the air in front of him. Sam wanted to see his face. The anonymity of the slave withheld too much of his power. She tore off his mask and a mane of blond hair fell to his shoulders. His square jaw was set impassively but his wide eyes betrayed his longing. That she had such a perfect specimen of manhood so totally under her spell made her quiver with delight.

She stood before him, teasing him. She ran the whip up her inner thigh, wrapping the tasselled end around her leg. The slave was transfixed. Sam then slid the handle into her vagina and slowly fucked herself.

'Oh yeah, mistress,' sighed the slave.

'Silence!' barked Sam, and with that she withdrew the dildo whip and stuck the handle into the slave's mouth.

The slave sucked greedily on her juices. She repeated the exercise a few times, easing the phallus into herself, covering it with the smells and taste of her sex, then ramming it deep into the slave's throat.

She was oblivious now to the stares of the onlookers, Marcus included. This experience was totally about her own pleasure. She fingered the brass rings hanging from the slave's nipples, first gently, then tugging hard. The slave gasped and said, 'Thank you, mistress.'

She wrapped the end of the whip around the slave's straining member. The leather coiled around his stiffened penis like a snake and she jerked the handle.

'Thank you, mistress.'

She undid the whip and lightly hit him across the chest, just enough to sting, just enough to warn him that she was still in control. Pre-come oozed from the end of his cock and Sam could feel the wetness of her own juices on her thighs. The slave stared lustfully at her crotch and she slapped him hard across his beautiful face.

'Ohh, thank you, mistress.'

Crouching, Sam nuzzled her face against his balls, her tongue darting out and licking the underside of his shaft. In that position, she lowered herself on to the handle of the whip. The slave was silent, knowing that to speak now could mean that his mistress might refuse to bestow her gift. Sam took his penis into her mouth. The slave bucked his hips and Sam bared her teeth, running them along the length of his shaft. He winced and grew still. From the way his penis jerked in her mouth, she could tell his orgasm was near. She let his penis slip out of her mouth and concentrated on fucking herself with the whip.

The slave looked on helplessly as Sam's hips gyrated on the leather phallus. She enjoyed the sight of a man wanting her so much and yet unable to do anything about it. Every now and then she would lick the head of his penis and then stop and return to her own pleasure. Faster and harder, she plunged the phallus into her sopping vagina. Her fingers slid across her clitoris. She was so wet. Rising and falling on the dildo, tonguing the cock that waved in her face, the friction on her clitoris increased.

'Please, mistress,' moaned the slave.

That familiar feeling began welling in Sam's loins. Knowing that she was about to come, she opened her mouth and the slave jammed his penis between her lips. As he did so, he came and the feeling of the hot salty liquid in her throat was enough to send her over the edge. Like a tidal wave, her orgasm engulfed her, taking her whole body and drowning her in sensuality.

She rested on her knees, exhausted. Now the pleasure had dissipated, she was aware again of the crowd that surrounded her. As if sensing her need, Marcus appeared, carrying her coat. He lifted her up off the floor, wrapped the coat around her shoulders and led her out into the night.

Chapter Five

SAM WAS SURPRISED when Martin Spencer phoned her the next day. He was ringing, he said, on the off chance that she might be free that evening and would be kind enough to do him the honour of accompanying him to a TV industry dinner. The old-fashioned way he asked for a date amused Sam and convinced her to say yes. It would be nice to be treated like a lady. She hoped that Martin was also old-fashioned enough not to expect any sexual favours. Martin seemed a little taken aback that she'd actually said yes and the conversation ended awkwardly after he offered to pick her up at around seven-thirty.

In the meantime, Sam had all day to worry about what to wear. She had been to this type of party often while at Walker, Rathbone and knew that they were just an excuse for industry bigwigs to get together and bitch about anybody who left the room. She also knew that the women there, from the wives of executives to the female executives themselves, would be dressed to the nines in their attempts to outdo each other and make sure theirs was the photo in the papers next day, shown casually getting out of their limousines in dresses to which they would, when speaking to the press, refer self-effacingly as 'this old thing'.

Sam opened her wardrobe and let out a sigh. There wasn't anything in there that was either suitable or that she hadn't worn to a hundred other occasions like this one. She needed a new dress, job or no job. But first she had to persuade her clothes consultant to go with her.

'Hi Judy, it's Sam. How's it going?'

'Frantic as usual. You sound much chirpier.'

Sam told Judy about the dinner party and how she needed her to go shopping with her at lunch time.

'Please, Judy,' Sam begged, knowing that her friend was weighing up how much work she had to do.

Judy always had been a soft touch when it came to Sam. 'Okay. I'll meet you at Bond Street tube in an hour.'

'Thanks, Jude. Oh, and one more favour – can you see if you can find out who will be at this thing tonight?'

Judy agreed to do her best and rang off.

Shopping, whether window or for real, was one of Sam's favourite pastimes. Her choice spot for clothes was the area between New Bond Street and South Molton Street. She gloried in the sun as she waited outside the tube station. She couldn't believe the summer they were having. The temperature had been over seventy every day and the warm weather made her unemployment just a little bit easier to bear. Everything suddenly went dark as two hands were placed across her eyes.

'Guess who?' giggled Judy.

Sam turned around and hugged her friend. 'Come on, we haven't got a minute to spare. I need a label fix.'

Grabbing Judy's hand, Sam dragged her off to her first port of call, her favourite, Yves St Laurent. She was like a whirling dervish whipping in and out of the changing room, lugging armfuls of clothing with her, her only conversation being to question Judy on her opinion of the latest item.

But before Judy could even finish her last comment Sam was shooing her out of the door and on to the next designer shop. They went through the same ritual in three more stores until Judy insisted they stop for a cappuccino. Sam reluctantly agreed.

'So have you found out anything about tonight?' asked Sam, as they sat down in the café.

'There'll be the usual industry bores. You know, the same old men who've pressed you up against the wall at a million other dinners to tell you how much they admire your work as they try to cop a feel.'

'Anybody else?' laughed Sam, sensing that Judy was building up to a revelation.

'One person who just might interest you.'

'Who?' asked Sam, sitting up straight.

'Guess.'

'You know I'm hopeless at this game. Male or female?'

'Female.'

Sam thought for a few minutes. She couldn't

think of any female that would really interest her, apart from royalty, and that was out of curiosity to see them in the flesh.

'Princess Anne?'

'No. But the rumour is that this woman also has a special relationship with horses,' said Judy, smiling lewdly at a passing waiter.

'Oh, I give up.'

'Harriet Bowman.'

Sam looked puzzled for a moment. Then it dawned on her, 'Marcus's ex!'

'That's right. Miss Harriet Bowman, daughter of Northern TV's chairman Sir Clive Bowman, former confidante of roguish but dashing millionaire Marcus McLeod, society glamour girl and part-time criminal.'

'Judy, you're outrageous. You know nothing was ever proved.'

'Not about the insider dealing, no. But I'm sticking by what I said about the horses . . .'

Sam paid the bill, her mind working overtime. If she spoke to this Harriet maybe she could find out more about Marcus. But in the meantime there were more shops to ransack. She hauled a protesting Judy to her feet.

Their first stop was Browns, where Sam fell instantly in love with a cream silk dress with a tight bodice top that flared out at the waist and came down to her calves. She knew it would be perfect even before she had put it on. She came out of the changing room and Judy wolf-whistled appreciatively. She had to admit it was the best thing Sam had tried on. Its colour made a stunning contrast to her black hair.

Not to be outdone, Judy then insisted that they

go to the Gaultier boutique. Sam nearly died of shame when Judy went into the changing room and emerged in a conical bra.

'Guess who I am?' said Judy and she began humming a Madonna song.

'Judy. You're not going to buy that?' asked Sam, laughing incredulously.

'No. I could have somebody's eye out,' Judy deadpanned.

Judy went back into the changing room. When she reappeared, fully dressed, she said, 'And the men of London collectively sigh with relief.'

They browsed around the shops for another couple of hours. Judy finally admitted defeat and they walked back to the tube station. Sam couldn't resist bringing up the subject of Harriet Bowman again.

'What do you think she's like?' she asked.

'Probably a snotty bitch.'

'I don't think Marcus would have bothered with her if she was like that. I wonder if I dare talk to her.'

'What on earth are you going to say?' asked Judy. 'Tell me, Harriet, what was Marcus McLeod like in bed?'

They both giggled at this prospect.

'No, I'd try to be a little bit subtler,' laughed Sam. 'Though I wouldn't have to if you were coming too.'

'Sorry, hon, but duty calls. I shouldn't really have come out this afternoon.' Judy kissed her friend goodbye and disappeared into the crowds.

Sam paced nervously up and down her flat waiting for Martin. She wasn't nervous about him or the dinner – she cared little about either – but the thought of meeting someone who knew Marcus intimately made her extremely anxious. At last the doorbell rang. As she opened the door, Sam gave Martin a perfunctory kiss on the cheek.

'Shall we go?' she said and led the way to the lift.

In the car, Martin struggled to make conversation but Sam paid him little attention, answering his questions in terse monosyllables. In the end, exasperation got the better of him.

'For God's sake, Sam, what's the matter with you?'

The tone in his voice made her come to her senses. 'I'm really sorry, Martin, I've just got a load on my mind. You don't happen to know Harriet Bowman, do you?'

'I do actually. Her father and I go back years. I've done a lot of business with him. Why?'

'We've got a mutual friend in common. Would you introduce us?'

'Sure. Who's the mutual friend?'

Sam guessed Martin knew the answer already. She knew he wasn't prying, just making small talk, but she didn't really think it appropriate to talk to him about Marcus. She looked out of the window to signal that the conversation was at an end. Martin gave up and resigned himself to the silence.

The car parked outside the hotel where the dinner was being held. As Martin opened the car door for her, she realised that although there were many other fabulously dressed women arriving at the same time, all eyes were on her.

'You look beautiful,' said Martin.

Sam blushed but secretly she knew it was true.

Once inside the banqueting room Sam was

grateful that the noise level made conversation between her and Martin all but impossible. He reluctantly left her side to fetch some drinks and she scoured the room looking for Harriet. The only pictures she had seen of her had been in the newspaper clippings, which were several years old. She'd looked overdressed and fussy in the photos – and that could have described many of the women in the banqueting hall – though she'd also had some indefinably exotic quality. She thought about approaching one woman in particular but then decided it would probably be better to wait for Martin to introduce them properly.

The dinner seemed to go on forever and there was one self-congratulatory speech after another. Sam didn't even try to make conversation with the other guests at her table. She'd overheard enough of their bons mots for one evening. She tried talking to Martin but her questions sounded forced, her laughter too brittle. She was growing irritated by the way he looked at her adoringly, hanging on her every word, and she realised that he'd completely forgotten the favour she'd asked him in the car. Finally she snapped.

'Have you seen the Bowmans this evening?' she said, interrupting him as he launched into yet another uninteresting story.

Martin looked hurt, aware now that she hadn't been listening to a word he said. 'What is it with you and the Bowmans?'

Sam could feel her cheeks go red. She was being unfair to him. She tried to sound conciliatory. 'Oh, it's nothing. I'm going to get another drink – would you like one?'

Martin nodded dolefully.

Sam stood up to go to the bar. One more drink and I'm out of here, she thought. It had been a mistake coming out with Martin. He was only trying to be nice to her and she was nastily cutting him dead all the time. She'd come out to be flattered but although Martin's compliments were profuse, she realised that flattery meant nothing if you didn't appreciate the person doing it.

She spotted the toilets and decided to freshen up. She loved the glamour of using the ladies' rooms in posh hotels, the expensive perfumes and soaps laid out around the marble basins and the subtle lighting which contrived to make even the plainest of women look like a movie star. Checking her make-up in the mirror, Sam thought that even Judy couldn't complain about her appearance under these lights. She reapplied her lipstick, even though it was near perfect, just to revel in the luxury a moment longer.

She could see another woman entering the room behind her. She blinked: it looked incredibly like Harriet. Sam shrugged off the idea – it would be too convenient. She checked her lipstick for bleeding and watched as the woman splashed some water on her face, then came and stood next to her. It was definitely Harriet. She had the same exotic, foreign look. The pictures had been black and white, which did little to show off this woman's best assets – her auburn hair, cascading in curls down her back, and her luminous, olive-green eyes. Harriet was supposedly English through and through, but Sam fancied that somewhere along the line, a strange mixture of Irish and Spanish had been added to the Bowman gene pool.

The woman caught Sam staring. 'Do I know

you?' she asked. Her voice was much softer than Sam had expected.

'You're Harriet Bowman, aren't you?'

'Yes I am. Have we met before?'

'No, but I think we may have a mutual friend in common – Marcus McLeod. By the way, my name's Sam Winterton.'

Harriet's face broke into a huge, warm smile – an expression that spoke volumes without a word being uttered. 'Dear, sweet Marcus. Such a lovable rogue. Are you seeing him at the moment?'

Sam was a little disappointed that Harriet hadn't heard of her, then realised she was being stupid. Harriet had just had a brief fling with the man years ago. Why should she have been interested in his subsequent affairs?

The surprising thing was, Harriet did seem interested in her, and Sam found herself telling this near stranger far more about herself than she'd intended. The woman seemed to have a way of drawing information out of her and Sam felt strangely captivated.

'Enough about me,' said Sam, realising she'd been talking for ages. 'Tell me all about you and Marcus.'

In any other circumstance she would have felt rude and nosey, but Harriet made her feel as though they'd known each other for years. Harriet gave her a sly look and agreed to her request.

'But not before,' she said, 'we steal ourselves a bottle of champagne.'

Back in the dining room, Harriet nonchalantly swiped a bottle of champagne from a passing tray while Sam looked for Martin. She spotted him and was relieved to see that he was in the middle of a heated conversation with several television producers and seemingly oblivious to her disappearance. The two women found a quiet corner in an adjacent lounge and sat down.

Harriet poured the champagne and lifted her glass. 'A toast to Marcus and all who sail in him.'

'Unfortunately, I haven't sailed in him yet,' confessed Sam. 'What's he like?'

'Ten out of ten,' said Harriet, 'for inventiveness, stamina and warmth.'

'What's the catch with Marcus?'

'That you can't catch him. That's his one big flaw. He's always moving on. But I don't really want to talk about Marcus. I'm more interested in you.'

Sam blushed at the attention but told the woman about her present unemployment and even about Toby. Harriet made sympathetic noises.

Her new friend was very modest when it came to telling her own story. The daughter of a very rich man, she had had the best of everything. A public school education, followed by Cambridge and then straight to work at her father's company, Northern Television, where she was now on the board of directors. Harriet made the whole thing seem like nepotism but Sam got the feeling that this woman could do anything she set her mind to. And shockingly at this moment she seemed to be setting it to seducing Sam. For with each glass she emptied, Harriet grew increasingly affectionate.

'So why is a stunning woman like you sleeping

on her own?' asked Harriet. 'Men must be queuing up around the block.'

Sam thought Harriet must be drunk because as she said this, Harriet slid her hand along Sam's thigh. Sam smiled at her, unsure of what was happening, and Harriet drew closer. Oh my God, she's flirting with me, thought Sam, feeling the heat of Harriet's breath on her cheeks. The bigger surprise was how much Sam was enjoying it. She felt mesmerised by this woman but she was uncertain how to handle it. Sam had pictured herself many times in her fantasies making love to another woman but it had always remained just that – a fantasy.

She took a closer look at Harriet's face and wondered what it would be like to kiss another woman's full, soft lips. Then her eyes alighted on Harriet's ample bosom, which her evening dress barely concealed. Sam imagined what her breasts looked like and what it would be like to suck her nipples. What would she taste like down there, between her long, elegant legs? How would it feel to have Harriet sucking on her clitoris whilst she returned the favour? Now she knew the score she would be brazen about her desires.

But before she could say a word, she heard her name being called. Martin! She turned to see what he wanted. He was pointing to his watch and mouthing that it was time to go. Sam wanted to tell him to go on his own but she felt guilty. It didn't make him look very good that his date had ignored him all evening, and to make matters worse had spent her time flirting with another woman.

'I'm afraid I've got to go,' sighed Sam.

A look of disappointment clouded Harriet's face. 'So soon?' she said, giving Martin a scathing look.

Sam wondered if she should offer her telephone number but decided not to, since Harriet made no mention of it. But then Harriet leaned over as if to whisper something to her but instead, she lightly bit Sam's earlobe, then kissed it. Sam felt a sudden jolt of pure lust.

'Sam.'

It was Martin again. The two women hurriedly hugged and said goodbye.

In the car home Sam was very quiet, partly out of annoyance with Martin breaking up the party and partly because she was deeply immersed in a fantasy involving Harriet Bowman.

It was the day of the Ladies' Final at Wimbledon. Sam could hardly believe that Marcus had managed to wangle two tickets for the best seats on centre court. Of course, it wasn't a simple day out – there was still the matter of a wager. This one was to be on the winner of the tennis match.

Marcus had been scrupulously fair and forewarned Sam of the bet so she could watch the whole of the tournament to check out the players' form. This was to counteract her accusation that Marcus had cheated on their first wager. She also had her doubts about his honesty in the second.

Sam was pleased that the player she thought was going to win from the beginning had made it to the Final and she had placed two thousand pounds on her at a bookie's. Marcus had escorted her, as she had never been into a betting office before. This was their first bet that was being carried out properly. Surprisingly, Marcus put his money on the same woman. In response to her question on what would happen if she didn't win, he said that as banker he would cover Sam's outlay. The odds on her chosen player winning were ten to one against.

Appropriately, Sam dressed in white: a long, cotton, fifties style dress with a flared skirt and in keeping with this, a small cotton cardigan and flat pumps.

The phone rang. It was Marcus ringing from his car to say he was downstairs waiting for her. She tied her hair back into a ponytail and took one final look at herself in the mirror. She looked so innocent all in white – she could have been that goody two-shoes girl in *Grease*.

A white stretch limousine with smoked glass windows was parked outside. Sam laughed at its trashy ostentation, while at the same time revelling in it. The chauffeur held the door open and she climbed in next to Marcus.

'You look fantastic,' he said, kissing her cheek.

The limousine silently glided away. Sam looked around in amazement. It was so large inside, there was almost enough room to lie out on the floor. In one corner there was a drinks cabinet and in the other, the latest in stereo equipment. Marcus switched on the tape. It was *Madam Butterfly*, Sam's favourite.

'How did you know . . .' she started.

Marcus interrupted her. 'I know everything there is to know about you.'

She sat back in her seat and relaxed, transported by the soaring music. Marcus busied himself with a bottle of champagne which had been cooling in the drinks cabinet. Thoughtfully, he had corked it just before she arrived. He poured her a glass.

'To winning and to love,' he toasted.

When they arrived, they made straight for a marquee reserved for celebrity guests. Sam was very excited at being so close to the rich and famous. She had to resist elbowing Marcus and pointing out the legendary actress and singer standing with her arm around her tennis player boyfriend. Marcus would think it incredibly uncool. But Sam, despite her success in the business world, had always been like a little girl around the famous, especially film stars.

The tannoy announced the start of the game. Sam was sitting very close to the action and even closer to the famous singer.

'What a perfect day,' she said softly to Marcus.

'And there's still the bet,' he replied.

Sam had almost forgotten about it. She hadn't even wondered what the forfeit might be as she had been so confident of winning, especially after Marcus put his money on the same player.

In the first set, it looked as if all was going well. The favourite had won 6:2. She started well in the next set but then her stamina started to go and her challenger, a woman almost half her age, started to move ahead. The set ended 1:6.

Sam was on the edge of her seat. Jumping up, she shouted, 'Come on, you can do it.'

Everyone looked at her and she quickly sat down again. Marcus just laughed at her enthusiasm. Still, if the woman lost it wouldn't make any difference to him financially, apart from covering the cost of her bet. And that was pocket money to someone like Marcus.

The final set brought Sam out in a sweat. Each player won alternate games. For a while they were stuck on deuce. But Sam's player just didn't have the energy to keep going and was finally defeated. It was game, set and match to her opponent. Sam couldn't believe she'd lost a bet again.

'Suspicious as I am over the first two bets, Marcus,' she said as they left the court, 'I don't suppose even you could fix Wimbledon.'

Marcus gave her one of his more enigmatic looks. 'Never mind, I want you to come and meet someone in the marquee.'

Marcus would say no more as he led the way. The tent was crowded and noisy with the sound of congratulations, commiserations and corks popping.

'Ah, there she is. Come and meet my dear friend Harriet.'

Sam thought she must be hearing things. 'Harriet who?'

'Bowman. I'm sure you must have read about her in the newspapers.'

Sam wanted some time to think. How was she going to handle this? Luckily, Harriet solved her dilemma.

'Harriet, this is Sam. Sam, this is Harriet.'

'Delighted to meet you,' said Harriet. 'I'm surprised we've never met before.' As she said this she gave Sam a surreptitious wink.

'It's nice to meet you too,' said Sam.

It was obvious that Harriet wanted to play along with Marcus by making out that she and Sam had never met. Sam remembered his words

'I know everything about', and doubted that Marcus was unaware of their previous meeting.

Marcus went looking for drinks and Harriet seemed to penetrate Sam with her eyes.

'You look so fresh and innocent today,' said Harriet, in a husky voice. 'Like someone who should be corrupted.'

Sam remembered how she had felt the last time they'd met; her fantasies of taking Harriet's clothes off and touching the soft flesh, a mirror image of her own body. 'And are you just the woman to do it?'

Harriet let out a low laugh, 'I sure am.'

Marcus returned with the drinks and some strawberries and cream. 'I'm glad to see you two are getting on well,' he said with a gleam in his eye.

It was hot and stuffy in the marquee and Sam was glad when Marcus suggested they take a drive in his limousine. She sat opposite Harriet and Marcus. There was about four foot of carpet between them.

Harriet was the first to speak. 'I find the smell of all this leather such a turn-on, don't you, Sam?'

Sam tried not to look at Marcus as she remembered their night at Pain. 'Mmm.'

Marcus saw to the drinks and Sam could feel the sexual tension welling up in the car. Harriet had lifted her dress up slightly so that Sam could see her white briefs. Sam couldn't help but stare. She wanted to see what was there; more importantly, she wanted to taste it. She felt too shy to make the first move, so she responded by copying Harriet, pulling her dress up and parting her legs slightly so Harriet could see what she was offering.

Harriet took a long look, licking her lips. To

further their cat and mouse game, Harriet undid the front buttons on her dress, revealing her majestic breasts, pushed up and parted by her bra. Marcus was staring at Harriet too but he made no move to touch her. Sam realised she had once again been slow on the uptake. Making love to Harriet was to be her forfeit, and as always, Marcus was just there to watch.

Sam, having no buttons, simply undid the zip and allowed the top of her dress to fall down. She wasn't wearing a bra and both Harriet and Marcus looked pleased as they studied her pert bosoms and erect nipples. For a moment, she felt inhibited about doing this in a car and she had to remind herself that although she could see out, no-one could see in. There was even a glass partition between them and the driver. All this would be for their eyes only.

Just seeing the lustful stares of her two companions made Sam wet. Her small, white cotton pants were drenched and she decided to take them off. She made sure that as she did so, her legs were positioned far enough apart for Harriet to see her sex. Harriet breathed deeper as she watched Sam remove her underwear. Sam stayed with her legs parted and her dress hiked up to her thighs.

Harriet went one step further and took off her dress completely. Sam admired her olive skin and the small red heart tattooed on her thigh. Harriet's high-legged knickers emphasised her extremely long legs.

Sam studied Harriet's crotch. It turned her on to see the outline of the other woman's labia and also to see the tell-tale signs of her excitement.

Like Sam, Harriet's pants were soaking. Both women seemed to forget that Marcus was watching their every move.

Having never been with a woman before, Sam was unsure of what to do next. Harriet sensed this and took charge. She slipped on to the carpeted floor of the car, steadying herself by placing her hands on Sam's knees and at the same time parting Sam's legs wider. Once balanced, she folded Sam's dress up to her stomach and at the sight of Sam's vagina, Marcus let out a long, low moan of appreciative lust. Sam enjoyed the sound of his excitement and wanted to please him and Harriet more. Using both hands, she applied pressure to her pubis, making her lips fold back and unsheathing her clitoris. It had the desired effect. Both Marcus and Harriet looked crazed with desire for her.

Harriet helped Sam take off her dress. Kneeling back, she admired Sam's body, running her fingers over Sam's torso, lightly flicking her hardened nipples, weighing her breasts in her hands. Then her fingers were replaced by her mouth and Harriet sucked greedily, moving from breast to breast as if unable to tell which one pleased her the most. Sam grabbed hold of Harriet's hair and drove her down, down to where a fire was raging.

As the limousine sped through the heart of London, Harriet's mouth played a delicious teasing game with Sam's vulva. First her tongue would feel soft, gently navigating the folds of Sam's labia, then it would harden, jabbing at her clitoris and sending jolts of pleasure racing through Sam's body. It was Sam's turn to moan.

She noticed how different Harriet's mouth felt compared to a man's. Harriet's lips were as soft as her own labia. Harriet looked up at Sam's face as she let her tongue run all over her vagina, seeking out every hidden place. The turn-on of seeing a woman do this to her was almost too much. The temptation to lie back and sink into orgasm was great but Sam wanted to return the compliment first. She was curious to know what it felt like to kiss a woman intimately, to taste her juices, to know the right places to make her come.

With the greatest of effort, she stopped Harriet's beautiful mouth.

'It's my turn,' said Sam, as she helped Harriet to lie out on the floor of the car, facing Marcus with her legs bent. Marcus had been silent for a while. Sam turned to him next. 'Take your cock out. I want to watch you play with yourself while you watch me fucking her with my tongue.'

Marcus did as he was told.

At first Sam licked only on top of Harriet's pants. She knew from her own experience the delightful sexual torment this created. She used her hands to stretch the material tight against Harriet's pubis, allowing both herself and Marcus to see how wet Harriet had become. Harriet tried to take her pants off, becoming desperate for Sam's tongue directly on her skin. But Sam brushed her hands away. She was in charge and she was going to savour every minute of this new experience.

Tormenting Harriet further she moved up to her breasts, feeling the firm mounds of flesh and the hard, erect nipples. Harriet lifted and ground her hips against Sam's as Sam moved up her body and started to kiss the mouth that had given her so much pleasure. She could still taste the saltiness of her juices which lingered on Harriet's lips and the smell of her sex on another woman drove her wild.

Marcus had unbuttoned his trousers to let his angry looking penis poke out through the fly. Masturbating slowly, he watched the women intently, keeping his rhythm the same as theirs. Sam couldn't wait any longer to look at Harriet's sex or to touch it properly. Even in a vehicle as large as this, there was a moment of awkwardness as she helped Harriet off with her underwear. The fuss was worth it.

Once again, Marcus moaned as he saw Harriet displayed before him. Sam caught her breath. Harriet's lips, like her own, were swollen with desire. Sam was fascinated at how different Harriet's vulva was compared to her own. The lips were larger and much darker and her clitoris seemed slightly longer.

As Sam studied Harriet's clit she knew she could not resist it any more. She leant forward and started to lick the hard piece of flesh, moving her tongue in circles at first softly and then increasingly harder. She pushed her tongue deep into Harriet, savouring the sweet smell – a different, slightly stronger aroma than her own scent. For a while both women were more than content to let Sam's tongue thrust deep into Harriet's vagina. But then Sam stopped and refocused its attention on Harriet's hard clitoris.

Harriet started to breathe faster as Sam's tongue pressed harder and Sam pushed two of her fingers into the wet orifice, wanting to get to the centre of Harriet. She shunted her fingers in and out as hard as she could while she built up the pressure on Harriet's clit.

Behind her, Sam could hear Marcus crying, 'Oh, my God.'

She knew Harriet was about to come as she was frantically rubbing herself against Sam's mouth and fingers.

'Don't stop,' screamed Harriet.

Sam felt Harriet's vaginal muscles start contracting around her fingers now wet from the juices spurting from inside. The woman's sex seemed to be squeezing every last second of available pleasure from Sam's probing hands. As Sam felt the contractions subside, she moved herself away. Her face was covered in Harriet's secretions, and she licked her lips.

Harriet lay back, perfectly still, an orgasmic blush covering her breasts and neck.

'That was fantastic. God, I'm trembling all over. Give me a minute to get myself together.'

Sam smiled at Harriet. 'Just relax. I've just noticed that our host hasn't come. I think I'll give him a show.'

Sam sat back on the seat opposite Marcus and spread her legs wide apart. She fingered the inside of her lips, stroking upwards to her clitoris.

Before going any further she spoke to Marcus. 'It's not going to take much to tip me over the edge. So watch closely, Marcus.'

Marcus's brown eyes burned with desire. As she began frantically rubbing her clitoris, Marcus picked up her speed, shunting his foreskin backwards and forwards, pounding his cock. Sam just thought of Harriet's wet, inviting sex, smothering her face, and she could feel the start of her own orgasm.

'I'm coming, Marcus. Now.'

Sam threw her head back, eyes closed, groaning with delight as both Marcus and Harriet egged her on while her sex burst into orgasm. As the sensation took over her body she could feel drops of Marcus's come raining down on to her legs. Opening her eyes again, she saw Harriet looking at her, her face still a picture of lust.

Chapter Six

STILL HALF UNDRESSED, Sam and Harriet curled up on the back seat of the limousine, one either side of Marcus.

'I don't want today to end,' said Harriet, drowsily. 'It's been absolutely perfect.'

Sam smiled across at her. 'I know what you mean. Does it have to end now, Marcus?'

Marcus put his arms around the two women and cuddled them.

'Of course not, my darlings. I've a surprise to finish off the day perfectly.'

Marcus wouldn't say any more. The two women tried to coax the secret out of him. Unbuttoning his shirt they each took a nipple into their mouths, playfully biting him, trying to persuade him to admit defeat and reveal his intentions. But in the warm afterglow of sex, the game was half-hearted and pretty soon the three of them were asleep as the car drove on in the balmy summer evening, making its way out of London.

Sam awoke to find a blanket had been put over

her. Harriet was on the floor of the limousine, laughing as he searched among the detritus of their debauchery for her underwear.

'God, I'm too old to be fucking in the back of a car,' she said, holding up her knickers and frowning at the sorry state of them.

'But what a car,' said Sam, stretching out. 'Where are we, Marcus?'

He was on the opposite seat holding a tumbler of whisky, looking immaculate as if the afternoon had never happened. 'Any second now we should be at my house.'

As he spoke, the car turned a corner and stopped in front of an imposing wrought-iron gate. The driver got out to attend to the security system and the gate groaned open. In front of them lay a long gravel drive leading to, somewhere in the distance, the Georgian mansion that was Marcus's country residence.

'Marcus, it's beautiful,' said Sam, glimpsing the floodlit house growing nearer.

'Catch,' said Harriet, throwing Sam's underwear at her. 'I don't think poor old Gould's heart could take it if he saw you get out of the car looking like that.'

'Who's he?' asked Sam, hurriedly slipping her pants on. Her once immaculate white outfit now looked a little crumpled, to say the least.

'The butler, would you believe?' Harriet arched her eyebrow.

'And here he is now,' said Marcus, as the car came to a stop.

An old man carefully made his way down the steps in front of the house and opened the limousine door just as Sam was pulling her underwear up on to her hips. He appeared not to notice. 'Good evening, sir. Ladies.'

Sam climbed out of the car feeling completely bedraggled. Harriet and Marcus followed on behind.

'Good evening, Gould,' said Marcus. 'This is Miss Winterton and Miss Bowman. Can you show them up to the guest bedrooms so they can freshen up? It's been a long day.'

The two women looked at each other and laughed. Harriet's auburn curls were standing up on end and somewhere she seemed to have mislaid a shoe. Sam realised that she herself was still holding on to an empty champagne bottle. Marcus looked at them with disapproval.

'We've been invited to a friend's house for dinner tonight but I don't feel you're quite dressed for the occasion.'

Sam and Harriet laughed even more.

'Somehow I guessed this might be the case, so I've taken the liberty of buying you both a little something to wear.'

Both Sam and Harriet looked intrigued.

'Lead the way, my man,' said Harriet, adopting a tone of mock grandeur.

Gould led the way, albeit at a snail's pace. The two women had to stifle their laughter as the old butler wobbled unsteadily in front of them. They entered an enormous hallway and Marcus quickly disappeared through one of the many oak doors that lined the cavernous room. Sam's laughter subsided as she took in her surroundings. In the middle of the hall there was a large hexagonal dark wood table inlaid with intricate marquetry, on top of which sat a crystal vase filled with beautiful white orchids. A glass chandelier swooped dramatically down from the ceiling, flooding the hall with light. The highly polished black-and-white chequered marble floor gleamed, as did every surface, a feat which impressed even a hardened clean-aholic like Sam.

At the end of the hallway there was a long marble staircase that went up one flight and then divided into two. Sam imagined herself being carried up that staircase by Marcus.

'Very *Gone With The Wind*,' she said out loud without thinking.

'I don't think Rhett Butler there's got the energy,' whispered Harriet, pointing to Gould.

The old man seemed impervious, both to their remarks and to the lavishness of his surroundings. Slowly he led them upstairs and showed them their rooms, which were next door to each other.

'If you need anything please do not hesitate to ring the bell. I'll be right along.'

Harriet shrieked and Sam nudged her discreetly.

'Thank you, Gould, I'm sure everything will be fine.'

The old butler set off again, even more slowly than before, seemingly exhausted by the execution of his duties.

Harriet opened her door. 'Come in when you're ready,' she said. 'I can't wait to see what you're wearing.'

The room was even bigger and more opulent than Sam had imagined. It was furnished with an assembly of period pieces, picked with Marcus's usual exquisite taste. In pride of place was a massive four-poster bed, the canopy and curtains of which were made from a heavy gold-threaded material with an Oriental design. A dark blue and burnt umber Madras check counterpane was folded back to reveal white silk sheets. Sitting on the bed and sinking into its softness, Sam guessed that four people could probably sleep in it comfortably. Although three would be enough, she thought, picturing Marcus and Harriet sharing it with her.

Out of the corner of her eye she noticed a clothes bag hanging on the handle of the wardrobe. Her outfit. She jumped off the bed and picked up the bag.

'What kind of dinner party is this?' she wondered out loud as she inspected its contents.

The dress, which was made from deep red velvet, consisted of little more than a push-up brassiere attached by several gold rings to the briefest of mini skirts. Also in the bag was a box containing a pair of high-heeled mules, and a note from Marcus which read:

Dear Sam, I hope you like the outfit. It should be a perfect fit as I think I should know every curve of your body by now. What I would like you to do after you've read this is to have a bath and wait until further orders. See you soon. M

Sam opened the door to the ensuite bathroom expecting to see a smallish room equipped sufficiently for a guest. What she found was fit for an Arabian Night's harem. The bathroom was easily the same size as the bedroom and the temperature was only slightly cooler than a sauna. The main feature in the middle of the room was the sunken marble bath, which had already been drawn, with rose petals scattered on top of the water. In fact the room was thick with the scent of roses and Sam noticed several little brass burners on the floor, warming liquids which were undoubtedly the finest essential oils.

Next to the bath sat a tidy pile of thick white towels and a matching bathrobe. Sam quickly stripped off her wrinkled clothes and slid into the bath. The water was a perfect temperature.

For about a quarter of an hour she lay back and let her mind empty. Every muscle in her body relaxed and she felt utterly serene, without a care in the world. Then she began to wonder what Marcus had in store for her. This was going to be a far from ordinary evening, if the dress was anything to go by.

As if on cue Marcus appeared in the doorway, wearing a bathrobe similar to the one laid out for her.

'How's it going?' he asked.

'I feel fantastic.'

He walked over to the bath and knelt down. Picking up the soap he started to wash Sam's back, moving around to her breasts. Sam felt tingly all over and wondered if at last Marcus was going to have sex with her. He told her to stand up. Building up a lather in his hands he started to soap her thighs and very slowly moved up to her vulva. Gently he washed her, his hand sliding around to her anus. Sam unconsciously parted her legs and Marcus bent forward to kiss her pubis. As he stood up again, Sam wiped the soap off his nose.

'What now?' she asked, hoping that Marcus would slip into the bath beside her.

'As you will have noticed, I left no underwear with your dress and that's because I want you exposed and ready for anything.'

As Marcus was telling Sam this, he let his fingers slide into her. She moaned at his touch and at the thought of being permanently exposed for him.

'But,' he added, 'at the moment I don't think you're exposed enough.'

'What do you mean?' Sam felt incredibly curious.

As a reply, he rinsed the soap off her, then manfully lifted her out of the water, wrapped her in one of the fluffy towels and patted her dry. Opening another door on the other side of the bathroom, he beckoned Sam to follow him. Inside was a smaller room tiled in white with a massage table at one end, and rows of glass shelves containing an amazing array of unguents and perfumes.

'Hop up,' Marcus told her, pointing at the table, 'and lie on your front.'

He selected one of the bottles from the shelves and unscrewed it.

'I think we'll stick with roses,' he said, pouring some oil into the palm of his hand. Slowly, he began massaging Sam's shoulders and she let out a small moan of pleasure. Building up the pressure, he moved down to her buttocks, kneading them and parting them slightly. Sam knew that he was looking at her anus. Next his hands were on her thighs, prizing them apart, and once again his eyes pored over her vulva. Frustratingly, he didn't touch her there, but as he massaged her legs, and then her feet, Sam became perfectly relaxed.

He told her to turn over and began to massage

her front. He spent several minutes on each breast, lovingly stroking her nipples. When he got to her crotch, he teased her clitoris with his finger.

'Marcus, please fuck me. You're driving me mad.'

'Don't be so impatient. I have lots of lovely things in store for you tonight.'

Marcus wiped his hands on a towel. As the massage seemed to have ended, Sam made to get off the table but Marcus said, 'I haven't finished yet.'

Sam suddenly felt a coldness between her legs. Looking down she saw Marcus was rubbing shaving cream into her pubic hair.

'Marcus, what . . .'

'As I said, Sam, I want you to be completely exposed. Nothing hidden,' he said as he picked a razor off the shelf.

Sam couldn't reply. She felt incredibly turned on and equally frightened. 'Be careful,' she said, finally.

'Of course,' said Marcus, with a glint in his eye. 'I'd never harm one hair on your head.'

Sam kept her pubic hair fairly short and so the razor glided easily through the little black patch on her pubis. Once that was bare, he moved down to the more delicate area around her lips. Bending her knees, he pushed her legs wide apart so he could see what he was doing. Sam knew he could see and even hear her wetness as he made sure her lips were out of the way of the razor. He was constantly touching her, thumbing her clitoris, as he painstakingly removed every hair. Sam felt almost insane with desire. Marcus seemed to ignore her sexual state, intent on finishing the job at hand. Finally, he took a damp cloth and dabbed at her crotch.

'There, I've finished. Don't move, I'll fetch a mirror.'

Sam thought she would scream if Marcus didn't relieve the sexual tension that was welling up in her.

He reappeared with a mirror and held it between her legs. She couldn't believe how different she looked. As she moved closer to her reflection she saw the intricate details of her crotch and her labia were much more prominent than she had expected. She could even see the hood of flesh that hid her clitoris. With her hand, she explored the newly uncovered terrain between her legs. There was no doubt she was now totally exposed.

Marcus put down the mirror and admired his handiwork, Sam shamelessly spreading her legs wide so that he could see every nook of her denuded sex.

'You look beautiful, Sam. I love being able to see every part of you like this. I can see your clitoris harden even as I speak.' As he said this, he let one finger slide between her open lips. 'You're wet again, Sam.'

'Don't stop, please,' she begged, clutching his wrist and forcing his finger inside.

But Marcus removed his hand, saying, 'There's no time. Get dressed. I'm sure Harriet can't wait to see how you look.'

He blew her a kiss and left the room.

Sam was equally keen to see Harriet. She returned to her bedroom and quickly put on her make-up and pinned up her hair. She felt nervous as she put on the dress. What if she looked dreadful in it? She needn't have worried; she should have learnt to trust Marcus by now. For looking at herself in the mirror, she had to admit, she looked stunning. Red was definitely her colour and the push-up bra made her breasts look round and full. She was aware of the skirt only barely covering her. One false move and the whole world would see what Sam Winterton had to offer, a thought that scared and excited her in equal measures. The shoes finished the look perfectly. She was ready.

She knocked on Harriet's door, shivering with anticipation. Harriet shouted at her to come in. Harriet was naked, towelling dry her hair. She turned as Sam entered and was almost speechless. 'Wow.'

'And that's not all,' said Sam, pulling up the small piece of material that was covering her crotch.

'All I can say is wow again,' said Harriet. 'You are one extremely hot little number.'

As Sam moved to Harriet's side, the woman nudged her on to the bed.

'Mind my hair,' said Sam, laughing, as a couple of strands came unpinned.

'What hair?' asked Harriet, as she put her mouth on Sam's labia. She licked each lip in turn, then almost roughly, she shouldered Sam's legs apart.

'You look so vulnerable, so sexy, so exposed,' she said, her luminous green eyes ablaze with desire.

'Exactly as our lord and master likes it.'

Harriet stopped talking and used her tongue to

fuck Sam's wet vagina. At the same time, she manoeuvred herself so that her own sex hung over Sam's face. Sam could feel Harriet lapping at her clitoris and she reciprocated in kind. Lick for lick until she was lost in a delirium where she felt it was her own clitoris that she was tonguing. The women's eager hands worked on each other, building the momentum, stroke for stroke until Sam felt she would burst.

Suddenly there was a knock on the door.

'Who is it?' shouted Harriet breathlessly, lifting her head up from between Sam's legs.

'It's Gould, ma'am. The master says can you be ready to go in five minutes.'

'Tell him to make it ten.'

'He won't like it, ma'am.'

Harriet sighed and jumped off the bed, leaving Sam high but most definitely not dry. 'Sorry, darling but His Master's Voice and all that.' Harriet looked in the mirror and threw her towel at Sam. 'It's all your fault,' she laughed. 'I haven't even put my make-up on yet.'

Sam got off the bed and stood next to Harriet to inspect the damage.

'Oh my God. I look as bad as I did when we got here. My lipstick is all over my face.'

'And elsewhere,' said Harriet, looking at her thighs.

For the next ten minutes the two women hared about the room, trying to make themselves look presentable. Harriet put on the dress Marcus had bought for her. Like Sam's dress, it too was made from velvet but there the comparison ended. The green dress had a high neck and came down to Harriet's knees. That wasn't to say it wasn't sexy.

It clung to every gorgeous curve but Harriet still looked like a nun in comparison with Sam.

'How come you're so covered up?' asked Sam, feeling a little less confident at the way she was so laid bare.

Harriet looked slyly at Sam. 'Because this is your fantasy, Sam. Marcus is out to fulfil all your desires. Believe me, I've had my turn. Come on, he'll be waiting.'

Sam and Harriet raced down the marble staircase, overtaking Gould on the way. As they ran past him Harriet lifted the back of Sam's skirt and the old man caught a quick glimpse of Sam's bottom.

'Harriet!' Sam laughed, despite herself.

'Oh come on. The old sod was probably standing outside the bedroom all the time we were in there.'

Marcus was impatiently pacing in the hallway. 'At last. Honestly, you girls, I never know why it takes you so long to get ready.'

'Oh, I think you do,' replied Harriet.

Again Sam sat opposite Harriet and Marcus in the limousine but this time she crossed her legs. 'I think you two have seen quite enough of me at the moment.'

Marcus laughed. 'Whatever you say. As I'm sure you've guessed, tonight we are going to have another wager. This one's very simple. All you've got to do is guess what the dessert's going to be but I think I'll risk a thousand pounds on your not getting it right.'

Sam had no idea and so to help her Marcus then told her what the other courses were going to be.

'I give up,' she said petulantly. 'Make it crème brulée. This is ridiculous.'

'Done,' said Marcus. 'Crème brulée sold to the knickerless woman opposite.'

They were slowing down. Sam peered out of the window and saw that they were approaching a quaint sixteenth-century ivy-covered cottage. The car stopped and the driver jumped out and opened the door. Sam was sure that he caught sight of her crotch as she stepped out. He certainly had a smile on his face.

A door opened and the pretty cottage garden was bathed in light. Sam guessed the man who came up the path to greet them to be in his early forties.

'You must be Sam,' he said, taking her hand and kissing it. 'You look wonderful. I'm Daniel.'

Sam smiled at him, noting that, despite his age, he had boyish good looks with a sandy fringe flopping over his clear grey eyes. His smile was both open and intriguing.

'And you must be Harriet. I think we've, er, *met* before. Quite a few years ago.'

'Yes, I think we did *meet* once,' replied Harriet.

Sam turned around to look at her friend but Harriet remained remarkably straight-faced.

'Marcus, it's great to see you after all this time.' Daniel gave Marcus a bear hug. 'And, as always, accompanied by such beautiful women.'

Sam felt a wave of jealousy. She quickly quelled it. Why was she upset? This wasn't a new revelation, for God's sake. Daniel ushered them all in to the dining room and Sam was surprised to see the table was set for ten. She had supposed that it would be a foursome.

'The other guests are here already in the garden. Go on out and I'll bring you drinks.'

The garden at the back of the house was floodlit. As they entered there was a hush as the other guests studied them, making Sam feel incredibly uncomfortable. Marcus broke the ice by saying hi to everyone by name. Sam was puzzled that he knew them all.

'Who are all these people, Marcus?'

'Just old friends. Come and meet Dominic and Zoe.'

As Marcus made the introductions, Sam was aware that the couple were staring at her and sizing her up. She knew that she was dressed provocatively but they didn't even hide their lust, which made the banal party chatter between them even more bizarre.

She was relieved when Marcus said she must meet the other guests. As they walked towards the end of the garden, she took in the scenery. The garden itself was as natural as the surrounding countryside. It appeared that plants and trees just grew where they wanted to. There was a small stream running through the bottom of the garden, where a couple, both blond, stood engrossed in each other. They spotted Marcus and Sam approaching and smiled as they said hello.

'This is David and his partner Jane.'

Sam chatted to Jane, a petite woman who had the good fortune to be able not to wear a scrap of make-up and still look incredible. After a few minutes of polite conversation about stockbroking, Jane excused herself to get another drink. Her partner broke off from his conversation with Marcus and came over to Sam.

'That dress does great things for you, Sam,' he said, moving closer.

Before Sam could even say thank you, David had put his hand on her breast. Sam glanced at Marcus who nodded, urging her on. She looked at David more closely. His blond hair and the smiling, green eyes reminded her of Toby. She put the still painful thought to one side as David touched the hem of her dress. With only a slight bend of his knees and an almost imperceptible movement with his hand, he brushed against the bare skin of her vagina.

He obviously wasn't expecting Sam to be shaved and a big grin spread across his face. 'I've got to give it to you, Marcus, you've outdone yourself.' He smoothed the bare skin of her pubis. 'You don't mind, do you?' he asked, as he fondled her lips.

Sam shook her head. She was terribly turned on, having this stranger touch her in the middle of a party. She could see that her vagina was driving him mad as his trousers had tightened perceptibly around his erection.

As he slipped his fingers into her, Sam spotted Jane coming out of the cottage clutching a tray of drinks. She was mortified. David had his back to the house and was unaware of his partner's approach. Sam went to move away but at that moment David turned around and called to Jane. 'Come and feel between Sam's legs. Marcus has shaved her.'

Jane's eyes lit up and she handed the drinks to Marcus who was laughing at the look of sheer terror that had crossed Sam's face.

'I love that feel,' said Jane, as she placed her hand where David's had been.

'Your hands are cold from the drinks,' replied Sam, jumping slightly. She felt disorientated by this turn of events.

'I think they're warming up pretty fast, don't you?' replied Jane, as she stuck three fingers into Sam's vulva, making her cry out.

Sam looked around to see if anyone had heard her or was aware of what Jane's hands were doing. It seemed no-one had noticed, not even Harriet, who seemed to be getting on very well with Daniel. Jane started to stimulate Sam's clitoris with her lubricated fingers while David moved behind and inserted two of his fingers inside her. Sam closed her eyes. Having David and Jane work on her like this was blissful. She even forgot she was in a garden full of strangers. She didn't want them to stop.

'Faster,' she instructed them.

They complied with her bidding but, within seconds, they were interrupted by Daniel shouting out that dinner was ready. The couple stopped and walked arm in arm with Sam back up to the house.

'I can't believe this,' said Sam.

Marcus put his arm around her. 'Never mind, the food's fabulous here.'

'Marcus!'

All Sam's frustration exploded in his name and he looked quite taken aback.

'Calm down, Sam. I'll make sure it's all right later.'

'I'm sorry. It would be an understatement to say I'm a little frustrated at this moment in time.'

Marcus laughed, breaking the tension, and escorted Sam back through the garden.

At the dinner table, Sam was placed next to Dominic and she discovered that he was a lawyer. His partner, Zoe, appeared to be having a heated conversation with Marcus over ethical invest-ment. Sam smiled inwardly. She didn't think Zoe was going to make a convert there. Dominic seemed happy making inane chatter, which was okay with Sam, as she wanted the chance to sort out her thoughts on what had just happened in the garden.

The first course was a delicious but ferocious clam chowder. Everyone around the table seemed deeply involved in their conversations and Sam wondered if they had a common bond other than Marcus.

'Do you all know each other well?' she asked Dominic.

'Yes, of course, we've known each other for years. Apart from you and Harriet.'

Sam looked across the table at Harriet, who was now feeding Daniel grapes.

'Harriet seems to know Daniel quite well,' she observed wryly.

'Yes, he told me earlier that it was quite a surprise seeing her turn up on his doorstep. He fucked her once at a polo match. He had no idea who she was.'

'Small world,' said Sam, with her eyebrows arched. 'So how did the rest of you meet?'

Sam caught him giving a sidelong glance at Marcus before answering. 'Um, well, Daniel here is a chef and he, um, started a dining club which we all joined.'

Sam was puzzled. 'What sort of dining club?'

'One with a common aim.'

Before Dominic could explain, Daniel interrupted them as he served the main course. Piling thin slices of duck on to Sam's plate and covering them in a dark, aromatic plum sauce, he turned to Dominic and said, 'I hope you don't mind, but could you swap with Ben? He says he hasn't even had a chance to say hello to Sam yet.'

'Sure. No problem. Speak to you later, Sam.'

Sam couldn't believe all the attention she was getting. It must be the dress, she concluded. Harriet was now sitting on Daniel's lap and stroking Marcus under the chin. What a woman, thought Sam. Harriet saw her looking, winked suggestively and blew her a kiss.

Ben got up from the other side of the table, leaving a seat vacant next to Francesca, his girlfriend, a loud, large-breasted woman with a short shiny black bob. Dominic sat down next to Francesca and promptly kissed her cleavage. Sam was startled but her attention was soon drawn to Ben. Like all the men at the table, he was exceptionally good-looking and in his late thirties or early forties. He was also dark-haired and dark-eyed, with a penetrating gaze that gave Sam butterflies. These people all seemed so shameless. She crossed her legs, not realising that her skirt was barely covering her until she followed Ben's eyes, which were fixed on the very tops of her legs.

'Do you mind?' he said as he lifted the skirt the necessary half-inch.

Sam knew there was no point in being modest and besides, she still ached with frustration. Ben looked immensely pleased when he saw that she was shaven. Pushing his chair back, he slid under the table and in between Sam's knees. Parting them he began to lick up her thighs until he finally reached the core of her. With his fingers he separated her lips and with the tip of his tongue he concentrated on her clitoris. Sam had to purse her lips to stop herself moaning out loud. She couldn't believe that no-one had noticed Ben's dis-appearance. A sigh escaped her, as Ben's tongue thrust into her sex. Francesca looked at her and smiled and went back to her conversation with Dominic. No-one was paying her a blind bit of notice.

Finally, she couldn't control herself any longer. As her orgasm grew near she held on to the tablecloth for support, accidentally knocking her wine glass over. Cold liquid poured off the table and between her thighs. She gasped at the sudden coldness of it and her face burned with a mixture of shame and passion. Ben responded by licking harder, revelling in the new tasted that mixed with Sam's sweet juices. As she came, she bared her teeth, desperately trying to keep control.

A few seconds later, Ben was beside her again, tucking into his now rather cold duck. If it hadn't been for the stickiness of her wine-covered thighs, Sam would have believed that she had imagined it all. For although the other diners were boisterous, Harriet especially, nothing untoward was happen-ing elsewhere.

Daniel came to clear the plates away. He acted remarkably innocent.

'Sam, you've knocked your glass over. Let me get you another.'

Either he's the best actor in the world, thought Sam, or I'm going mad. 'Please,' she said shakily.

Daniel refilled her glass and said, 'And now I have a wonderful new dessert for you all. But I have a feeling that one or two of you have sneakily tried it already.'

And with that he produced a blindfold and tied it around Sam's eyes. The other diners whooped. She heard Marcus's voice. 'I'm afraid, my darling, you were wrong again. The dessert isn't crème brulée, Sam, it's you.'

For a moment she fumed, her ego having taken a dent at having been outwitted by Marcus yet again. Then she relaxed and began to laugh. The wonderful thing about betting against Marcus was that she never really lost whatever the outcome.

'You're a bastard and a cheat, Marcus,' she said as Daniel helped her up from the table.

Daniel warned her to duck as they passed under a low exposed beam and she was taken into what she guessed must be the sitting room. She could hear the rest of the dining club following on behind her. At first nothing happened, and the room went very quiet. Then Sam became aware of a hand, gently stroking her back, then another one, taking down her top and stroking her breasts. A tongue played with her nipple. Four hands were stroking her legs and she could tell from the softness that one pair belonged to a woman. The hands went as near to her crotch as they could without touching her sex. It seemed as if all the people touching her were in collusion to make Sam as desperate for sex as possible.

Suddenly there was a hand on her vagina. Sam could tell it was a man and was surprised when the person did nothing more. Just as she was going to say something, Marcus spoke. 'You're going to have to get to fever pitch, Sam, before we'll satisfy you. We know that you've been pleasured once already this evening and now we want to know that you are burning again.'

'You know I am, Marcus. Please don't torment me any longer,' she begged.

Marcus laughed and Sam realised it was his hand on her. He slowly slid a finger into her but then withdrew it.

'I don't think you're ready yet,' he said, and she could sense that he had moved away from her.

Before she could say anything else, several people were helping to take off her dress without disturbing the blindfold. Sam savoured the eroticism of so many unseen hands working on her body and the delicious anticipation of where they were going to touch her next. This temporary lack of sight brought a whole new dimension to sex. All of her other senses became much more acute. She could hear the individual breathing of people and she knew that some people were screwing each other a short distance away. Her skin felt so sensitive she was sure that she recognised the touch of Harriet on her breasts. And she was certain Ben was behind her from his body smell.

Someone then helped Sam to sit down and arranged her legs so her vulva was exposed, open and inviting. No-one came near her for a few seconds and then she felt a penis scraping against her mouth. She engulfed it and was aware that her sense of taste was also much stronger. She licked up and along the shaft, nuzzling the tip and cupping the balls in her hand. She decided she would give as good as she was getting and instead of satisfying the thrusting cock, she just teased it. She heard Dominic's voice.

'Marcus, I'm sorry. I can't wait any longer.'

Marcus must have given him a signal because the next moment he picked up Sam and laid her over the arm of a leather Chesterfield. Kneeling down behind her, he reversed the roles and started to stroke her labia with the end of his cock. Sam backed on to him. She was burning, desperate, and exposed – all of the things that Marcus wanted her to be. Dominic thrust his cock into her as hard as he could. He was so excited that after only a few more jabs, Sam could feel the warm stickiness of his sperm shooting into her. He withdrew and moved away.

She was disappointed but not for long. Harriet came and sat down next to her. She gently stroked Sam's bottom.

'You looked as though you really enjoyed your duck. Are you disappointed that you didn't actually get any dessert?'

'I'm sure you can think of something,' Sam said, as Harriet fingered the come running down Sam's thighs.

'Funny you should say that,' said Harriet, lifting Sam further over the arm of the sofa.

Sam could feel an inanimate object against her labia. At first she thought it was a vibrator but then quickly realised from its shape, as Harriet pushed it into her, that it was a banana from the dining table. Sam was aware that, at this angle, the other guests could see Harriet fucking her with the banana in every intimate detail. At the same time, Harriet was tormenting her clitoris in the way only she knew how. Sam begged her not to stop but Harriet took out the banana and said, 'I'm sorry, I've got my orders.'

Harriet got up off the sofa. Sam was desperate, the sexual tension inside her raised to fever pitch. Then, another hand, this time male, stroked her sex.

'I'm going to fuck you.' It was Ben.

'Please,' said Sam, in a small voice.

Ben helped her off the sofa and she crouched on all fours on a rug. Immediately he entered her, sliding in easily with the combination of her wetness and Dominic's come. He called to Francesca and Sam was soon aware of the woman beneath her, licking her nipples. Before she had the chance to savour this new sensation, another was upon her.

A penis brushed gently against her lips. The head was huge and dripping, wet with the unmistakable odour of Harriet's vagina. Another pang of jealousy hit Sam as she thought maybe it was Marcus in front of her and that he had already done to Harriet was Sam was desperate for him to do to her.

'Suck it.' It was Daniel.

Sam opened her mouth and the enormous head slipped inside. Backwards and forwards, she shunted, skewered on the two cocks thrusting at each end. She could feel Francesca's tongue, now on her clitoris. The thought of Francesca watching her partner's member as it drove into its target soon eradicated all thoughts of jealousy from Sam's mind. She guessed Francesca would be masturbating as she watched this exhilarating sight.

Sam felt more hands on her body. Fingers explored the walls of her sex as Ben's penis lunged between them. Hot mouths found her breasts, then moved away to be replaced by new ones. Now a man's tongue replaced Francesca's and the sucking of her clitoris became more insistent. All around her were the erotic sighs of people satiating themselves on her body. She was burning, desperate, exposed and finally satisfied as the two men poured their come into her and her own orgasm burst like a dam, flooding every inch of her body with erotic delight.

As her orgasm subsided, Sam ripped off her blindfold to see Marcus sitting naked on the sofa, far removed from the action, come splattered across his hairy chest.

'One day, I will have you,' she shouted, as she sank into the mass of writhing bodies and the whole thing started again.

Chapter Seven

SAM LAY IN bed, savouring the peace and quiet of being on her own. Stretching, she thought that she needed only one thing to make her feel completely satisfied – someone to go and make her some freshly ground coffee with some croissants and jam. Unfortunately, she was going to have to get up and do it herself.

It was another gorgeous summer's morning and she took her breakfast out on to her balcony. She half read the Sunday papers while watching the antics of a group of Japanese tourists as they photographed each other photographing the bridge. What if one of them knew Toby, she mused. It was a ridiculous thought and she turned her attention back to her newspaper. Reading through the travel section she thought about booking herself a holiday. She knew, practically speaking, that she shouldn't have one. However, it was almost too tempting to resist. She needed a break, a new perspective on her situation.

She had arranged to meet Judy for lunch at a

pub further down the river to discuss her options. Engrossed in an article about the Maldives, a destination out of her financial reach, she forgot about the time. Then, realising in a panic that she was going to be late, she had a quick shower and dressed in some old jeans and a T-shirt. She had planned to walk to the pub but now there simply wasn't time. Neither was there any time to put on make-up. Grabbing her car keys, she checked her reflection in the hall mirror and decided she'd pass.

A group of men were sitting at a table outside the pub and their heads turned as Sam drove up in her silver Porsche. They responded predictably to the combination of a fast car and a beautiful woman. Ignoring the whistles and the stares, she went into the pub and out the back on to a verandah which overlooked the water. Judy was already there in sunglasses, wearing a white chiffon blouse knotted over a slinky white mini dress. Spotting Sam, she pursed her shockingly red lips and tapped her watch in mock indignation.

You're late and your spritzer has gone flat,' she called out.

Sam sat down and took a sip of the drink that Judy had bought her. It was fine. 'Men are so bloody obvious,' she said. 'You don't have to be a psychologist to read their tiny minds.'

Judy didn't bother to respond. She and Sam were in perfect harmony on the state of the male mind and when she'd arrived earlier she'd been forced to give the finger to the same group out front. 'You're looking well and relaxed,' she said instead.

'I'm beginning to feel a lot more laid back about Toby's disappearance. As I've said before, who'd trust a man further than you or I could throw him? Besides, there's always Marcus to look forward to.'

Judy tried to interrupt her. Sam had been far too reticent about the mysterious millionaire.

'And before you ask any questions, the subject of Marcus is completely off limits today. I want to talk about this new man of yours.'

Judy had met a broker from one of Walker, Rathbone's rivals and was conducting a somewhat hush-hush affair. Although the company wasn't actually able to dictate to its employees about their private lives, such a liaison would have not been viewed favourably.

Judy's face broke into a big grin. 'Alan is fantastic. I'm meeting him later.'

'Where's he taking you?' asked Sam, tipping her head back to feel the sun on her face.

'To new heights in the bedroom, hopefully. Though we've been at it all night already.' She took off her sunglasses. Her eyes were nearly as red as her lips. 'As you can see, I haven't been getting too much sleep lately.'

'Any chance of getting away?'

'Funny you should mention that. It just so happens that I'm spending next week in New York. Alan's got a few meetings to go to. They're talking about a merger or something. I intend to check into Macy's on the Monday morning and be dragged out kicking and screaming on the Friday afternoon.'

'Lucky you. I've been thinking about going to Greece for a few days. On my own, may I add,' sighed Sam. 'I've worked out that I can just afford it if I go on a coach and take a packed lunch.'

Judy looked embarrassed. 'There I go again being so insensitive. I shouldn't be crowing.'

'Don't worry about it. I'm really pleased for you.'

'You won't be when I tell you who Alan's meetings are with.'

Sam frowned. She knew instantly who Judy was talking about. 'It's Julian O'Connor, isn't it?'

Judy put her hand on Sam's knee. When Judy had first met her, Sam was still reeling from her disastrous attempt at making a new life for herself in New York with Julian. 'Look, I'm not going to meet him. But if you still think it's a big betrayal I won't go to New York.'

Sam knew that Judy meant it and she felt touched by her friend's loyalty. 'Don't be stupid. It was such a long time ago. I stopped having those dreams about him falling down an elevator shaft at the World Trade Center years ago. So how is the conceited prick?'

Judy laughed. It was good to see Sam really feisty again. 'Well, there's good news and bad news.'

'Ooh, bad first,' said Sam.

'The bad news is, workwise he's doing really well and is, by all accounts, fabulously rich.'

Sam booed loudly, startling a sour-faced woman at the next table who had been trying to listen in to their conversation. 'And the good news is?'

'Well, Alan was told this in the strictest of confidence, so I'm trusting you to tell absolutely everybody. The good news is . . . ' Judy paused

124

for dramatic effect. ' . . . Julian is impotent.'

'Hooray!' Sam cheered and clapped and the woman at the next table looked away in disgust.

For the rest of the afternoon, the two women dished the dirt, their stories growing more lurid and more hysterical by the minute. When the barman called time, they walked back to their cars and were both relieved that the group of men was no longer drinking outside. Judy opened the door of her Volvo estate, a car which represented a clutch of values – family, safety, reliability – that were the complete antithesis of its owner. But as Judy often admitted, she loved that car as if it were human.

'You take care,' she said. 'I wish you'd tell me what Marcus is planning.'

Sam kissed her friend goodbye. 'I don't know myself.'

Judy waved as she drove off and Sam got into her own car, which in many ways symbolised freedom and escape. The first she already had, the second she was determined to get.

Sam had been to New York on numerous occasions but, she had to admit, never in quite so much style.

'Would you like some champagne, ma'am?'

Sam looked up at the air steward. 'Yes. That would be great.'

'What about your companion?'

Poor Marcus, exhausted from a lengthy takeover battle, snoozed while leaning against the window.

Sam smiled. 'I think it's best to leave him.'

She was quite happy to have a couple of hours

on her own. She wanted to appreciate every minute of this trip. When Marcus asked her to accompany him to New York, it couldn't have come at a better time. The four days on Crete could wait.

Her excitement had started from the minute Marcus announced that, naturally, they would be travelling on Concorde. When they had got on the plane Sam had been amazed at how narrow it was. Once they were airborne, it seemed hard to believe that they were going around the world at the speed of sound, the only proof being that they arrived in New York four hours after leaving London. Barely enough time for Sam to finish the in-flight magazine.

A limousine was waiting for them outside the airport to take them on to their hotel in Manhattan, a stone's throw from Central Park. From the picture window of their penthouse suite, Sam looked across the city and marvelled at the view. The roof of the Chrysler Building, her favourite, gleamed in the sunlight, while in the distance, the twin towers of the World Trade Center were covered in a misty haze. Seeing the building made her think of Julian and she laughed.

Everything was perfect. Apart from Marcus, who seemed to be very far away.

'What's wrong, Marcus?'

'Nothing. Don't you like it here?'

'Of course I do. But you seem so distant. Don't you want me here?'

'My dear Sam, please don't ever think that,' said Marcus, taking her in his arms. 'It's just that I've got to be really on the ball, workwise, for the next couple of days. I've got to conserve my energy. Once these meetings are out of the way, I'm all yours. Or you're all mine as the case may be.'

He kissed her on the cheek and told her to go shopping while she had the chance, then presented her with her very own gold Amex. She was blissfully happy until Marcus then told her that he would be sleeping away from her in another room in the suite. His excuse was that he would be working late and he didn't want to disturb her. Sam didn't believe him but she said nothing. The messages Marcus sent out were very confusing and left her feeling very rejected.

The mad shopping spree that she went on for the next three days helped alleviate that feeling. She barely had time to stop for lunch as she raided the stores on Fifth Avenue. Top of her list of purchases was underwear – she wanted to be prepared for anything that Marcus might come up with. As a balance to this rampant materialism she visited the Guggenheim and the Museum of Modern Art, where, as she looked on a mound of earth optimistically called, 'Revelation No. 3', she decided that either she must be a complete philistine or someone was playing a huge joke.

On her third afternoon, she stopped off in SoHo where she hoped to find some pictures within her price range. She found a gallery specialising in old black-and-white photographs and bought an aerial shot of the Chrysler Building taken shortly after its completion. Then, knowing that Marcus wouldn't yet be out of his meeting, she went on to a vegetarian restaurant in the East Village for dinner.

One of the many things Sam loved about New York was how it was divided into different areas catering for different needs. The Village was buzzing with exotic life, full of society's outsiders each dressed in their own individual uniforms. The area was a melting pot of hippies, punks, grungies, students, musicians and performance artists. Sam sat back, enjoying her meal and the spectacle being enacted in front of her.

It was nine o'clock when she got back to the hotel. She was surprised to see Marcus there already as she had hardly seen him in the last two days.

'Hi, how are you?' he asked, as he gave her another chaste kiss on the cheek. The lack of sexual tension stung. What was wrong with this man? She had now done things in front of him that she hadn't even imagined before meeting him, yet they never seemed to get over this barrier.

'Fine. What are you doing back so early?' She tried not to, but some of her unhappiness showed in her voice.

'My business has been satisfactorily concluded. It's time to party.'

Sam breathed a sigh of relief but kept silent.

Marcus continued. 'Have you ever been to Las Vegas?'

Sam admitted she hadn't.

'Well, in terms of our agreement I thought, what better place to go? I've just got to sort out the plane.'

He strode purposefully into his bedroom. Sam could hear him on the phone to a casino in Las Vegas. It transpired that they had a private jet on stand-by to fly out their more important customers and Marcus was undoubtedly important. It was soon all arranged: the plane would pick them up from an airfield just north of New York the following morning.

'Shall we order room service and have an early night?' he asked Sam.

Eagerly she said yes, in the hope that things were looking up. But after they had eaten and finished off a bottle of wine. Marcus suggested they go to their separate beds. Sam nearly cried with frustration.

She tossed and turned for several hours trying to understand him. Finally, she thought about Las Vegas and the possible scenarios he might have planned for her there. Although annoyed at what had happened in New York, she couldn't help but be excited about the trip to Las Vegas. She wondered if it was as tacky as her friends had told her. Eventually, she drifted off into a fitful sleep.

The flight there was uneventful, if glamorous, but every now and then Marcus would jump up and use the captain's radio, although he wouldn't tell Sam what it was about. They touched down in Las Vegas and the afternoon sun seared into Sam as they left the plane. It had been hot in New York but this desert heat was something else and she felt relieved when they stepped into the air-conditioned limousine.

Driving along Las Vegas Boulevard, Sam could hardly believe her eyes. One huge glitzy hotel after another, each with a more ludicrous theme than the last. They passed a thirty-storey mediaeval castle, a pyramid, a Roman palace and a hotel with what appeared to be a volcano outside. It was tawdry and lavish all at the same time.

'I'm speechless,' said Sam.

'Wait until you see where we're staying,' laughed Marcus.

Indeed, glitziest of all the hotels was the Raj. In keeping with its name, the golden domed building had been designed to look like a pink stone Indian palace. As their limousine stopped at the entrance, two Sikh doormen rushed over to them, shooing peacocks out of their path as they went. Sam got out of the car and tried to keep a straight face.

'Welcome to the Raj, Miss Winterton,' said the doormen in unison, bowing deeply. 'May all your dreams come true here.'

Sam effected a dramatic curtsey and walked into the hotel. She could hear Marcus laughing behind her.

He joined her in the lobby.

'It's a bit over the top,' whispered Sam.

'Just a little bit,' said Marcus. 'There were quieter places we could have stayed but I thought you'd enjoy the full Las Vegas experience.'

As Marcus spoke there was a roar behind them. Sam spun around to see, behind a glass wall, two tigers tearing into a hunk of meat. Sam was dumbstruck. As she looked around the lobby she saw that no-one was the least bit interested in this extraordinary spectacle. This was probably because most of the guests were a spectacle in themselves.

The hotel's guests seemed to divide into two categories – the rich and the fat. Sam had never seen so many obese people in one place.

Scattered around there were a few anorexic looking rich women of the type she knew all too well in New York. She hated that gaunt, brittle look, as the women who possessed it normally lived up to their image. But the alternative on display here didn't seem to be any better: hugely obese women with thirty years out-of-date hairstyles, decked out in luridly coloured polyester sundresses which were in most cases also given a sprinkling of sequins for good measure. A lot of these women carried buckets and as one waddled past Sam, she spotted that they were full of quarters, obviously intended for the slot machines.

There were also several brides milling around looking nervous and Sam saw a sign giving directions to the hotel's 'Temple of Love', which Sam guessed was the wedding chapel. Another sign pointed to 'The Jungle' and as the tigers roared again, Sam had no doubt that the sign meant what it said.

All of the hotel employees were Asian, the men dressed in white Nehru jackets and the women in multi-coloured saris. As soon as Sam and Marcus reached the reception, where a palm tree sprouted miraculously from the middle of the desk, people rushed around to welcome them, asking if they needed anything, carrying their cases and escorting them to the hotel's best suite. Marcus tipped them all handsomely and ordered room service to bring smoked salmon sandwiches and champagne.

Once inside their suite Sam threw herself down on a circular bed. She studied the ceiling, which was decorated with swathes of material encrusted with jewels and tiny mirrors. The bed itself was hand-carved and covered, in sharp contrast to the rainbow of colours around the rest of the room, with the purest white linen.

She propped her head up on her hand. 'Do you come here often, Marcus?'

He paused from unpacking. 'A few times a year. It's got the best casino in Vegas and probably America. More importantly, they always look after me. They get me anything I want.'

Sam sensed something in the last sentence that applied to her in some way. 'What are our plans while we're here?'

'I think we should rest for a while. I'll order dinner to be sent up, then after that, well, wait and see.'

He set about unpacking and Sam could tell that the conversation was over.

She explored the rest of the suite. There was something overdone about the lobby but their accommodation was exquisite. She checked out the bathroom and found that all the surfaces were carved from a cool white stone. A glass door led out on to a balcony adjoining the lounge. She walked out on to the balcony and was again hit by the force of the heat. She stood there for a while but it quickly became unpleasant and she returned to the lounge and sank into a soft plump sofa. Walking about the suite, she had realised much to her delight that there was only one bedroom and one bed. She hoped that this was a promising sign.

The next thing she knew Marcus was gently shaking her awake.

'Sam, dinner will be here soon.'

She looked up and saw Marcus standing in front of her, freshly showered and putting on a white shirt. She yawned and curled up tighter on the sofa.

'I'm tired,' she said.

'I know. The heat can really knock it out of you. But come on, get into the shower, we've got a lot to do this evening.'

Sam threw a cushion at him. 'Okay, okay.'

She turned the shower setting to 'Massage' and jets of water shot out from all angles, pummelling her body. Tonight, she thought, tonight it's definitely going to happen. The thought of what lay in store thrilled her and, feeling revived, she burst out of the shower and walked naked into the bedroom. Marcus was adjusting his bow tie in the mirror. He looked so distinguished and sexy, he took Sam's breath away.

'I love a man in a DJ,' she said as she walked up behind him.

She could see from his reflection that he was struggling with his emotions. He turned around and grabbed her wrists. For a while he just stared at her body, his face a mixture of desire and confusion. Shaking his head, he said, 'Go and get ready. Wear the long, backless, black dress.'

Sam looked flabbergasted. 'I just don't understand you.'

'Sam, please don't spoil things.'

There was a knock at the door and Marcus looked relieved to be able to get away and avoid this confrontation. Sam dressed quickly and went out on to the balcony where dinner had been served. Marcus stood up and hugged her. 'Don't be cross with me,' he said, kissing her neck. 'I've

133

explained all this to you before. I love you too much. I know it's hard to understand but just accept it for now and let's carry on with our little adventure.'

She leaned on the balcony wall and looked down on to the Boulevard, saying nothing.

The sun was beginning to set and it was now that Las Vegas really came into its own. What had looked tawdry in the daylight, now dazzled with a million neon lights. It wasn't quite beautiful but there was something about it that electrified Sam.

'It's quite a sight, isn't it?' said Marcus, reading her thoughts.

Sam gave in. Here was Marcus giving her the best of everything and she was being petulant about the one thing she couldn't have. And by being sulky her chances of getting that one thing were becoming more remote. 'Marcus, it's perfect,' she said, throwing her arms around him, trying to convince herself that she meant what she said.

Over dinner Marcus revealed that they were going to have another wager. He looked at her, smiling. 'I thought we'd just have a simple card game. Black Jack, perhaps.'

'And how are you going to manage to cheat on that one, Marcus? Will you have a spare deck up your sleeve?' she asked, laughing.

'You're so suspicious. I give you my word it's all above board.'

Sam looked at him sceptically.

'And before you ask,' he continued, 'I'm not telling you what happens if you lose.'

For the rest of dinner they talked about nothing in particular, as if they were a normal couple, while the sun set, casting a red glow over the desert sky.

As they got out of the lift, Sam couldn't believe the cacophony of noise coming from the thousands of one-armed bandits as the wheels whirled round and the dollars fell out. The same type of women that Sam had seen in the lobby, sat unsmiling at the slot machines feeding in quarters, their polyester sundresses replaced by more spangly evening versions. She thought it strange that, even in a hotel as expensive as this, they catered to the lowest common denominator. She was glad to escape the noise when they walked into the casino proper.

Here there was a hushed excitement as people gathered around the roulette tables and poker games. Vast piles of chips, representing thousands of dollars, were being raked nonchalantly across the green baize tables, to be lost on a single throw of a dice or turn of a wheel. Lots of people nodded or said hello to Marcus as they walked through the room. The waitresses, busily ferrying a constant stream of drinks to the gaming tables, appeared, to Sam, to be especially friendly towards him. Marcus smiled back but hardly seemed to notice their flirtatious manner. On the far side of the casino there was a small private room. It was here that some seriously large sums of money were won and lost. An attendant standing outside ushered them in.

'Everything is as you ordered, sir,' he said, closing the door behind them.

Inside, Sam was surprised to find that the dimly lit room was fairly spartan. There was one round card table similar to the ones in the main casino and two simple wooden chairs. On a silver tray on the table, there was a pack of cards and a decanter full of whisky with two glasses. They sat down and Marcus poured them both a glass. Sam gulped hers back in one go to quell a slight jitteriness. She wasn't sure if this was nerves or excitement.

As Marcus poured her some more, the door opened again and ten men, all dressed in dinner suits, walked in and lined up against the wall. None of them was Asian so she guessed that they weren't hotel employees. From their physiques and near flawless faces, she assumed they were models. She appraised them admiringly and then it occurred to her that Marcus might be expecting her to sleep with all of them if she lost. She knew she had managed, what was it, four, maybe five the other night? – but this was a new proposition entirely. She looked at Marcus quizzically, waiting to be enlightened.

'As you know,' said Marcus, shuffling the cards, 'the aim of the game is to get a score of twenty-one or as near as possible without going bust. I will be the dealer. We will play for money for an hour or so. After that, the stakes are far more precious as you'll be playing for the jewel between your thighs.'

Goose pimples rose up on Sam's arms.

'The number you bust by is important, as it is corresponds to how many of these charming men get to fuck you. Is that understood?

Sam just nodded.

Marcus unwrapped a paper roll containing some chips. He gave some to Sam, pointing out that the ten red ones she had were worth a thousand dollars each, the twenty yellow chips five hundred each and the numerous blue ones, fifty dollars apiece. Marcus dealt the first hand and Sam couldn't believe her eyes when she turned over the cards. She had an ace and a ten – twenty-one.

'I'll stick and I bet five thousand dollars,' she said, as she hurled five red chips into the middle of the table.

Marcus dealt himself another card. Then he smiled as he looked at his hand.

'It looks like you may be lucky this time, I've bust.'

For the next hour Sam's luck held out and she amassed more blue and red chips than she could count. Then, as she raked in the chips from another winning hand, Marcus announced, 'Be careful, Sam, we're no longer gambling for money.'

She looked at the men who stood motionless against the wall facing her. They remained entirely silent and blank-faced. Sam had no idea what they thought of her, a woman who was prepared to take on all ten of them. Maybe they assumed she was a prostitute. It was an unpleasant thought, and her hand trembled as she picked up her two cards. A four and a jack. She decided to stick. A wise move, as Marcus had a hand worth twenty. For ten minutes, Sam played extremely conservatively, neither winning nor busting.

'Come on, Sam, this isn't like you,' said Marcus, refilling her glass and lighting a cigar. 'Let's have a little bit of adventure here, a sense of danger.'

Sam ignored his taunts. She was sure that he

would be more than happy for her to bust by ten. Marcus shuffled the pack and then dealt again. Her new hand come to thirteen. Throwing two red chips forward she said with as much confidence as she could muster, 'I'll buy another card.'

Grinning, Marcus gave her the card. Nervously, she turned it over and her heart sank. It was a king. She had bust by two!

She threw the cards face up on the table and Marcus whooped.

'I think you can be proud of yourself,' he said. 'Not only have you made a lot of money tonight, you also get to have two of these gorgeous men service you. And I think, as you played so well, you get to pick.'

Sam quickly downed another whisky for courage and walked over to the men.

She appraised each man as if she was at an identity parade. It was a hard choice. How do you choose between different versions of perfection? In the end, she picked the first and the last man in the line-up. They could have been brothers. Both were swarthy six-footers with short, black hair, heavy brows and dark brown eyes.

Sam, Marcus and the two men left the room and walked in silence through the casino, past the polyester dresses still feeding money into the slot machines, and took the lift to their suite. Once inside the bedroom, Sam stood awkwardly, waiting for what was going to happen next.

'I'm going to sit here,' said Marcus, pointing to the chair placed at the bottom of the bed. 'Christian and James are here to service you but they are also in charge. You will be doing what they want. Okay?'

Sam nodded, feeling that familiar sensation welling up from between her thighs. Although she pretended otherwise she trusted Marcus implicitly. He would never let any harm come to her and she was willing to surrender to his desires.

Christian and James took off their jackets and untied their bow ties, before coming over to Sam. Christian stood in front of her and Sam waited, expecting him to kiss her or at least say something. Instead, he reached out and ripped the thin material of her dress to expose her breasts. She let out a scream. The dress had cost over three thousand dollars. She went to speak but Marcus motioned her to remain silent. James moved forward and finished the job off, throwing the torn dress on the floor. It became obvious that neither was going to speak to her. James indicated that he wanted her to take off her shoes. Sam complied. The two men then took an arm each and lifted her on to the bed.

Standing at the end, just in front of Marcus, they slowly began to undress each other. First came their shirts and Sam watched them, fascinated, as they touched and licked each other's nipples. From the bulge in his trousers, she could tell that Marcus was also aroused.

As the two men took off their trousers, Sam could see that both of them were sporting large erections. Christian slipped his hand under the waistband of James's white underwear and released his large, iron-hard cock. Sam wasn't expecting his next move, for Christian then crouched down and took James's penis into his mouth. Sam had never seen two men together before and she was turned on by the sight far more than she would have imagined. James grabbed Christian's head and jammed his cock into the back of Christian's throat. Sam watched intently, entranced at the aggressive nature of their sex. Christian's mouth was taking a pounding but both remained silent apart from the occasional animalistic grunt.

James withdrew and turned to Marcus. In a dramatic gesture, he dropped to his knees. Marcus sat bolt upright in the chair as James slowly undid his trousers and released his cock. James moved around to Marcus's side and then began to fellate him expertly, making sure Sam could see every movement he made with his lips and tongue. Marcus started to writhe and sigh. Christian knelt back and watched them both.

It took Sam some minutes to come to terms with the fact that Marcus was being sucked off by a man and enjoying every minute of it. In all her fantasies about Marcus she had never pictured him like this. But it thrilled her. She relished this strange new sight and soon her hand was busy at work between her thighs. First she rubbed her crotch through her knickers but the sensation wasn't acute enough and she slid out of her underwear and slowly stroked her clitoris, waiting for her turn.

As if reading her mind, Christian tapped James on the shoulder and pointed at Sam. James took the hint and moved away from Marcus. Marcus nodded and urged them on. Both men stripped off the rest of their clothes before getting on the bed with Sam. James put his arm across her breast and pushed her down on to the bed. He began to explore her mouth with his tongue and Sam could taste Marcus on him. As he kissed her passionately, he massaged her breasts with his big hands, squeezing her nipples and digging his nails into the soft mounds of flesh.

Between her legs, Christian was also putting his mouth to good use. He had his hands around the back of her knees and was holding her legs wide open. Christian was a pro, knowing all the tricks that would make a woman ecstatic. One minute he would tease her clitoris, using his tongue like a feather until she writhed with excitement. It was deliciously unbearable. Just as Sam thought she would scream, his tongue would harden and dart into her vagina, lapping noisily on her juices.

Christian and James were a brilliant double act. Sam almost believed that their tongues were synchronised. Sam had been to bed with two men before but it hadn't felt like this. Then it had been awkward, with each man nervously sizing the other one up, clumsily trying not to touch each other as if their masculinity would crumble if it were to happen. Christian and James had nothing to prove and Sam surrendered herself to their expert ministrations.

As if by prior agreement both men stopped what they were doing. James then helped Sam up, so that she was kneeling on all fours. She knew that behind her, Marcus now had the best view of her exposed, wet sex and she could hear his heavy, laboured breathing. Sam expected one of the men to slide into her but instead James moved underneath her, thrusting his cock into her face as his mouth pressed against her vulva.

She craned her neck to see Marcus rubbing himself as he watched James pleasuring her. Satisfied that Marcus was enjoying this sight, she turned her attention back to the cock beneath her and let it sink deep into her mouth.

By her side, Christian had started to rub her buttocks, prizing them gently apart so that both he and Marcus could see her anus more clearly, then he rubbed his finger around the tight hole. Leaning forward he began to lick around the rim and press his tongue just inside. Sam could hardly believe the sensations she was feeling as these two tongues penetrated her every secret place. And to top it all, Marcus could see everything. She bucked her hips, forcing both tongues to go deeper, wanting them to search further inside her.

Christian's tongue became more insistent as James frenziedly licked her clitoris. Sam began to shout at them.

'Oh, fuck me. Fuck me.'

The tongue in her anus was replaced by Christian's finger. She flinched momentarily at the pain, but the hurt soon disappeared, replaced by a feeling that drove her mad with sexual longing. Christian then began using two fingers, stretching her wider. Again, the initial pain and then the heightened sexual feeling. James had slowed down on her. Again the feathery touch on her clitoris. James knew just how to take her to the brink of orgasm and then stop, preventing her from coming and driving her on to new heights of pleasure. Sam was only dimly aware of Marcus; her sole attention was now on her own satisfaction. She thought she would explode if they didn't let her come soon.

Once more the men stopped in unison. Christian produced a tube of lubricant and began spreading it all around her anus. Sam looked up to protest. Sensing her apprehension, James stepped up his rhythm so that the sensations coming from her sex overtook what was happening to her anus. Then he grabbed her hair and forced her mouth to take his cock.

Suddenly, she felt the head of Christian's now greasy cock against her anus. She screamed as it pushed through the tight ring but again the pain was quickly over. Slowly but forcefully the shaft of Christian's member slid into this virgin territory. When its full length had been reached Sam could feel his balls slapping against her vulva. To match Christian's steady rhythm, James's tongue increased its speed and his cock thumped into Sam's mouth, bruising her lips.

As her orgasm began, Sam thought she was going to die. She bit hard on the penis that filled her mouth then released it and began to whimper. Every part of her body was undergoing a different sensation.

'Oh my God, oh my God.' She let out a massive scream that reverberated around the room as her knees buckled and she slumped on to the man beneath her.

Christian lifted her up again and spoke for the very first time. 'We haven't finished with you yet, Sam.'

She looked at them, dazed. She felt spent – what else could they want to do to her?

James slid out from underneath her and turned around, forcing her to sit on his cock. Her sex was now so wet and open, she had no trouble accommodating it up to the hilt. James thrust a few times and then stopped. Sam wondered if he was trying to prevent himself coming but it wasn't so. The lull was to allow Christian to slide into her anally once again and she felt the two cocks grinding against the thin wall between her anus and vagina.

The two men began to fuck her mercilessly. As one cock withdrew, the other forced its way in, building the friction on her vaginal wall, a new, unbearably pleasurable sensation. Her clitoris, tender from James's tongue, scraped against the man's muscular stomach. Christian and James slammed into her, their movements now united, thrusting at the same time, sending Sam into an orgasmic delirium. As she screamed out even louder this time, she heard Marcus's voice over the top of hers urging the men to fuck her even harder. As with everything they had done so far, they did it in perfect accord and, as if on cue, they both shot their come into her.

Chapter Eight

THE FOLLOWING EVENING, Sam still felt completely drained. Every muscle ached and she felt as if each of her limbs had been stretched to breaking point. There were bits of her that hurt that she hadn't even known existed. Still, it was all good exercise, she concluded, as she ran herself a bath.

Lying back in the sweet-smelling bubbles, she thought about the options open to her, workwise. She had now contacted almost every decent stockbroker's in London and all had come back with the same reply; none was recruiting at present. Ruefully, she wondered if she should have gone to Japan with Toby. She probably stood a much better chance of getting a job there at the moment. But even if she managed to find a job in Tokyo, the fact that Toby still hadn't contacted her spoke volumes about the durability of their relationship.

Toby. The thought of him caught her off guard. It was like that all the time. She really had to concentrate not to let him into her head. It was better when she was busy but the second she tried to relax, he'd be there. She'd lied to Judy that Sunday afternoon when she had said that it was getting better. She had been so convinced that Toby was the right man, the one who wouldn't be like all the others, the one who wouldn't let her down.

All the plans they had made together – everything seemed to point to a long-term future. It was too painful to think that he'd been stringing her along just to get into her bed. And the point was, if all he'd wanted was a brief fling, she would have been happy to have gone along with it. She'd wanted to sleep with him every bit as much as he did with her. Early on in their relationship she'd been in control of her emotions enough to keep it on a purely sexual level. But Toby had wanted more.

After so many disastrous affairs, it was she who had been the more reluctant to let her heart get involved. Toby had no such qualms and did everything he could to win her over and assure her that he was the right person for her. Eventually his persistence paid off and she surrendered, letting herself fall deeply, irrevocably in love.

The future was all mapped out, right down to the farmhouse they'd one day buy, where they'd bring up their children safely away from the confusion of the big city. Everything was accounted for except for the part where he walked out of her life and just disappeared. I'll always be there for you, he'd said. Trust me. She'd looked deep into his green eyes and she'd seen that he'd meant it with all his heart.

She ran some more hot water and wiped away a tear, not even bothering to pretend to herself that the shampoo had got into her eyes. With Toby the future had been filled with magical possibilities. She'd been on her way to the full set – the perfect lover, a great job and somewhere in the offing was the dream home. Now look at her. The first two had gone and it wouldn't be long before she wouldn't even have her flat. She was on the brink of bankruptcy. When she had taken out a mortgage, it had never occurred to her that in five years she would be unemployed and paying for a flat that was worth almost a third less than she had bought it for.

She had to find a job, quickly. Maybe she'd have to consider something other than stockbroking. Fleetingly, she thought about being a high-class call girl, something along the lines of *Pretty Woman*. Obviously there would be a Richard Gere character. Marcus? Sam laughed and scrubbed at her face as if to wipe away this ridiculous prostitute fantasy.

Sinking deeper into the water, she smiled as she wondered what her old careers teacher would have said if she'd told her that her ambition was to be a hooker. At school, most of Sam's teachers had made her their pet project. Despite coming from a poor family with no academic track record whatsoever, Sam had been something of a star at school, always top of the class in every subject. Her teachers believed that she was heading for Oxford, but Sam had known that she wanted to be out in the real world, not stuck in some ivory tower living on Pot Noodles. Having been poor she was determined to earn big money, to give her mother what she deserved. Sam's father certainly hadn't. Neither her mother nor Sam had grieved when he died.

It wasn't hard to figure out why she was so attracted to Marcus. Their backgrounds were very similar and they were both extremely ambitious. And the age difference, although not great, did make Sam look on him almost as a father figure. Back when they first met, they could have had the perfect relationship. If Marcus had been able to make love to her back then, she wouldn't be sitting in her bath crying over Toby now.

Marcus put his head round the bathroom door.

'Hi. Feeling rejuvenated and raring to go?'

'Not quite yet,' Sam admitted. 'Every muscle and limb in my body aches.'

'A little bit more exercise will put that right,' he said, coming into the room and sitting on the edge of the bath.

'To tell you the truth, Marcus, I never knew it was possible. Having anal and vaginal sex at the same time, I mean.'

'I'm glad to have taught you something new,' he said, splashing water at her.

He knelt at the side of the bath, rolled up his shirtsleeves and warmed his hands in the water before placing them on Sam's breasts. As he massaged each one he told her that he thought her breasts were perfect. She smiled and sighed as he pinched her nipples. Leaning over her he pulled out the plug. They both watched the water level sink, revealing more and more of Sam's body. Marcus traced a finger all the way down one leg.

'As they say, your legs are so long they go all the way up to your bottom,' he said, smirking.

'What a line,' said Sam, lightly flicking him with her hand. 'I mistakenly thought I was getting a bit of class with you, Mr McLeod.'

'But I am classy, Sam. I'm the best.' As the last of the bubbles drained out, he asked her to bend her knees and open her legs. 'And this is the best as well,' he said, as he placed his hand over her sex.

Sam shunted forward, eager for him to increase the pressure of his fingers. But Marcus moved his hand away and instead reached for the shower attachment on the taps. Turning it on, he kept the water running on his hands until it reached the right temperature, then pushed Sam's legs apart so that they touched the sides of the bath and placed the shower just above her vagina. At first, he washed away the last of the bubbles around her labia. Once this was done he separated her lips to reveal her clitoris and held the shower so the water ran directly on to it.

The sensation was intense. Sam could feel, almost immediately, the beginning of her orgasm. She watched the intent look on Marcus's face as he moved the shower head around so that the water would stimulate her even more. Before she could say anything she came. She expected Marcus to stop but instead, he redirected the jet of water on to her stomach for a few seconds and then moved it again between her legs. Again, barely had the water touched her clitoris than she had come, this time more intensely.

'Are there any tricks you don't know?' she asked, as Marcus brought her to her fifth orgasm.

149

'I know how to give you pleasure and that's what I intend to do. How many times would you like to come before we go out gambling?'

Sam looked as if she was seriously considering this. 'I think another five times will do nicely, thank you.'

'Your wish is my command, my lady.'

Sam lay back, concentrating on the tingling that was running from her groin, up through her stomach and playing around her breasts. The gentleness of the water meant the orgasms were painless. There was no build-up of soreness from friction. She thought she could go on having orgasms ad infinitum.

She wondered if Marcus wanted her to touch him. She made a move towards him but he gently held her back.

'I just want to serve you at this moment in time. So lie back and enjoy it.'

As Sam started to come again she felt quite happy to acquiesce to Marcus. 'I don't think I've ever had this many orgasms in one go,' she said, as she tenderly played with his hair. 'You're going grey, Marcus.'

'It's from all the work,' he said, pausing for a second, 'that I put into making my women friends sexually happy.'

'If that's the case I'd really like you to . . .'

Before she could finish, Marcus put his finger on her lips and began to play with the water on her clitoris again. She looked into his deep brown eyes and saw the sadness that he tried to hide. She shivered, wondering what was the matter with him.

After her tenth orgasm, Marcus turned the shower off.

'One more, please,' begged Sam, clutching the sides of the bath in ecstasy.

'You'll have to wait until later now. Anyway, you're starting to look like a prune,' he replied, laughing.

Sam looked at her hands and saw what Marcus meant. She had certainly been in the bath too long.

He hugged her and told her to get ready for their night of gambling.

'Is there going to be a forfeit tonight?' she asked.

'No. This is purely for money. Remember, there was meant to be a serious financial element to our agreement. Tonight you will be betting against the house.'

Sam looked puzzled. Why had Marcus not arranged a forfeit? Was he getting bored with her already and now only interested in winning money? Before she could voice her worries, Marcus shooed her into the bedroom where he had put out her long red halter-neck dress. He had even gone as far as choosing her jewellery, plumping for chunky geometric gold earrings and a matching necklace.

Sam spent longer than usual getting ready. She wanted to make sure that she looked perfect for Marcus, even putting on blue eye make-up to emphasise her limpid blue eyes. She couldn't stand the thought that he might be getting bored with their arrangement.

As she walked out of the bedroom, Marcus took a deep breath, 'You look beautiful. Come here and give me a twirl.'

Sam did as he asked. 'I meet with your approval?'

'In every way. Red is definitely my favourite colour on you.'

Sam smiled, happy that Marcus was happy. Perhaps she was just being paranoid about everything. Listening to him, he didn't sound like a man who was bored.

He held out an arm for her to take, saying, 'Let's go and win some money.'

In the casino Sam was staggered by the amount of money Marcus handed over in exchange for a small pile of plastic chips. Nonchalantly he gave her a handful worth ten thousand dollars. Sam felt slightly panicked.

'I can't take this much,' she said. 'What if I lose?'

She remembered a similar feeling she'd had as a small child. Every year her mother would take her to the seaside, normally Hastings, for their summer holiday. At the beginning of the week there would be the ritual of the handing over of the 'pennies envelope'. This contained a small amount of money which was Sam's to spend as she pleased in the arcades over the week. Sam knew how hard her mother scrimped and saved for this annual holiday and the responsibility to spend this money sensibly weighed heavy on her. This early lesson in economic management had stood her in good stead for later life. She was somewhat frightened of wasting anyone's money, no matter how rich the benefactor.

Marcus sensed her concern. 'You know as well as I do,' he said, taking her hand and leading her towards a roulette table, 'that I can afford for you to lose this and much more. This is a gift from me. It gives me great pleasure to have you with me.

Now, just play.'

There were five men and one other woman playing the table and it was obvious from the numerous chips in front of each of them that none was gambling a pittance.

'Five thousand on black seven,' said Marcus, his voice full of confidence.

Sam desperately wanted to put her chips on the same number but was worried that Marcus would think her stupid simply to follow him. Timidly she tossed a chip worth a thousand dollars on to the red twenty.

The croupier turned the roulette wheel and a few seconds later threw in the ball. The wheel spun around, the ball diving in and out of the numbers. Sam clenched her teeth, unaware that she was also wringing her hands. At the last minute she couldn't bear to look and screwed up her eyes. She couldn't believe her ears when the croupier shouted red twenty.

Losing her cool, Sam squealed with delight. 'I can't believe I've won,' she said, as she hugged Marcus.

Marcus looked amused. 'Why do you act so surprised – as if you have never gambled before? Surely you've learnt something over these last few weeks?'

'I know. But it's different tonight. With no forfeit I feel I should really be trying to win some money. God knows, I need it.'

'Let's play on then.'

For the next half hour or so, luck seemed to be with Sam on the roulette table. Her gains were great, her losses small. The other players had given up all pretence of lack of interest and were openly staring at her. Marcus, too, looked on proudly, as if he were responsible for this good fortune. But Sam still couldn't shake off her feeling of unease. 'I want to stop in a minute, Marcus, before my luck changes and I gamble all my winnings away.'

Marcus pushed some more chips forward. 'One more time.'

Sam reluctantly agreed, placing five thousand on the black five. She still found every go as nerve-wracking as the first, although she hid it better now, controlling her shouted outbursts. The wheel seemed to spin interminably. She willed it to stop. It slowed down and the ball rolled lazily into a number. The black five.

Sam screamed with excitement, flinging her arms around Marcus's neck. She felt a pure rush of adrenalin and briefly considered having another go.

'I think the gods are shining on me tonight,' she said, kissing Marcus's ear.

'Well, let's put it to the test. Do it again,' said Marcus, goading her on.

Fortunately Sam's good sense prevailed. 'I think the best gamblers know when to leave the table.'

'I'm glad you said that. C'mon, let's go upstairs.'

Sam looked closely at Marcus. Did this mean what she thought it meant? As usual, Marcus's feelings and thoughts were fairly impenetrable, although she sensed he wanted her. They went back to their suite in an awkward, expectant silence.

Once in the room, Sam walked over to the

154

dressing table and began taking off her jewellery, wondering what she should say to Marcus. She certainly didn't want to be rejected again. As she fiddled with the clasp of her earring she was unaware of Marcus walking up behind her until he lightly placed his lips on the bare flesh of her shoulder. She could feel his hands looking for the zip of her dress. Every muscle in her body tensed with anticipation. It was unbearable. At long last Marcus was going to make love to her.

He found the zip and in one quick movement had the dress off, leaving her standing in her underwear. Still standing behind her, he put his hand under her chin and gently lifted her head so that she could see herself in the dresser mirror. She watched, fascinated, as his strong hands moved on to her breasts. For a moment he let his hands smooth over the lace of her bra. Then, edging his thumbs into the cups, he uncovered her breasts.

He pinched and massaged Sam's nipples, all the while kissing the nape of her neck, murmuring that she was the love of his life. He was pressed up tightly against her and she could feel his erection pressing into the small of her back. She remembered the other night when James took Marcus's penis in his mouth, how erotic she had found that sight, seeing Marcus so vulnerable to another man. She had adored Marcus's cock from first sight. The length, the width; for her, it was perfection. She loved how straight it was and she desperately wanted it deep inside her, fucking her to the limit.

Marcus rubbed up against her and as she thought of him screwing her mercilessly, she became conscious of the wetness between her legs. She looked down at herself in the mirror and saw the damp patch spreading in her knickers. As if Marcus had noticed, too, he moved his hands down to her crotch, lightly playing with her labia through the wet material. Sam moaned with pleasure and frustration. She didn't want any more foreplay, she just wanted him to bend her over the dresser, rip off her knickers and impale her with his cock. She silently willed him to do this, grinding her buttocks even harder against his erection.

It didn't work. He stopped and told her to lie on the bed. She did as she was told, all the time watching him as he slowly undressed, almost taunting her as he revealed his body. Sam held her breath as he took off his boxer shorts. His big, perfect cock sprang out, strong and stiff, and it was all she could do to stop herself from jumping up and jamming it into her mouth.

Naked, Marcus knelt on the bed before her and eased off her knickers. Then he parted her legs and began to lick her thighs, stopping every now and again to admire her vulva.

'I've seen the most intimate part of you exposed so many times over the last few weeks and I never get used to how beautiful it is,' he said, dipping his head into her crotch.

With his tongue he began to trace the outline of her labia and Sam wanted to beg him to fuck her. As fantastic as the sensations he created with his tongue were, she knew they would pale to insignificance beside the actions of his cock. She desperately wanted to be opened up and filled by him but she sensed it would be better to let him take the lead. Marcus was not a man who could be ordered about.

He sucked on her clitoris, pulling it out of its sheath, slightly bruising it from the force. Sam winced but the pleasure took over from the pain. Sitting up, Marcus inserted one finger into her, watching her sex intently, fascinated as her lips opened further to let in another two fingers. With his other hand, he exquisitely massaged her hardened clitoris. This drove her over the edge. She was too turned on and wanted him too badly to remain silent.

She leaned forward and grabbed his cock. 'Please, Marcus, take me now,' she cried, feeling frenzied. 'Fuck me. I'm going to explode with frustration. Fuck me. Now. How many times do I have to ask you, beg you even?'

Marcus didn't even look at Sam as he pushed her away from him.

'Always my impatient little Sam,' he said, trying to smile. 'You can wait a little longer, can't you?'

She lay back in a sulk, unsure that she could.

He leant across her to the bedside cabinet. Opening a drawer, he found a ten inch, flesh-coloured dildo.

'Don't worry, Sam, I'll make sure you're filled and satiated.'

Sam stared at the dildo. There was no way it would fit inside her.

'Spread your legs. Further.'

Sam silently obeyed. At first, Marcus played around the entrance of her sex with the tip of the dildo. Despite herself, Sam found herself responding to the cold rubber and unconsciously she thrust towards it. Marcus took the hint and slowly drove the dildo into her wet, open vagina. The width of the dildo stretched Sam to her very limits. She could feel the tautness of her lips as they were forced further and further apart to allow the dildo to go deeper into her. Marcus looked hypnotised as he watched the rubber phallus disappearing.

'I love seeing you opened up like this,' he said, his voice husky with desire.

'I'll do anything for you, Marcus, you know that, don't you?' replied Sam.

'I should hope so, after all we've been through.'

The sensation overwhelmed her. She was aware that she didn't want this substitute for Marcus and at the same time she didn't want him to stop.

'Fuck me harder,' she pleaded, wanting the dildo, wanting him.

Marcus obliged. He built up a steady rhythm and then bent forward to lick her clitoris. His tongue was soon going in time with the dildo and it wasn't long before Sam came. Lost to the feeling, she momentarily forgot that this orgasm was not what she wanted or at least not how she wanted it.

As her orgasm ebbed so Marcus slowed down with the dildo until they were both perfectly still. For a moment they both just lay there in silence. Then Sam eased the dildo out of herself, feeling almost as if her body had betrayed her by responding so fully to this imposter. She jumped up and straddled Marcus.

'This isn't over yet,' she said, forcing a smile.

Marcus looked almost scared and he tried to make a joke of it. 'Are you never satisfied, Miss Winterton?'

'Never,' replied Sam, as she leant backwards,

without looking, to take his cock in her hand.

She froze when she felt Marcus's limp penis. Once she had got over the shock, she began moving his foreskin forward and back to restore his erection. There was no response. She then turned herself around and took his cock in her mouth. There was a slight stirring and nothing more. Marcus brushed her aside.

Sam felt she was about to cry. The rejection stung her. 'What's wrong, Marcus? Why can't you fuck me? Please tell me,' she said, her voice breaking.

Marcus looked close to tears himself. 'Leave me alone, please, Sam. I need some time to myself.'

Sam looked as if she was going to argue but thought better of it. Her temper rose, hiding the sadness. 'Fine. Suit yourself,' she said, as she moved off the bed.

She went into the bathroom and slammed the door. She looked at herself in the mirror. She looked dishevelled, her long black hair standing up on end with wisps glued to her face with sweat. Her cheeks were very red, more, she thought, from anger than from the sex. She brushed her hair violently, thinking about what had just happened. What was wrong with Marcus? He wasn't impotent; she knew he'd fucked hundreds of women, Harriet included. She wondered if it was something she'd done – maybe she'd been too demanding, too forceful. But that was ridiculous. Marcus wasn't the kind of man to be put off by a strong woman. Harriet was hardly a shrinking violet.

Sam's thoughts were interrupted by the sound of panting coming from the bedroom. Opening the door slightly, she saw that Marcus was masturbating. Once again he had a hard-on. As he wanked he cupped his balls with his free hand. Sam thought about going back into the bedroom. She still wanted her sex to take the place of his hand. But Marcus had a faraway look on his face. It was a private, detached moment. She knew if she went to him now, it would only compound whatever the problem was.

She felt tormented by the sight before her and yet she was transfixed. Despite herself she could feel that she was becoming aroused again. Almost shamefully her hand went to her crotch. As she slipped two fingers into her vagina she realised how much the dildo had stretched her. She felt sore but the sight before her in the bedroom excited her to the point where she didn't care. Juices oozed from her vagina and she lubricated her fingers and stroked her clitoris.

She knew that Marcus didn't intend her to see him. He was locked almost furtively in a very private moment. Sam couldn't take her eyes off him. She listened for every sound that escaped under his breath. She could tell from his moans when he reached a plateau and then pulled back, stopping the furious pumping of his hand for a second to let the feelings subside. For the first time Sam gained some sense of the thrill of voyeurism. She could see how exciting it was to watch from a distance as somebody gave themselves up to pleasure. Marcus was for the first time exposed to her.

His next move sent shock waves racing up from between her legs. As his hand built up speed and he began bucking his hips, he grabbed hold of the dildo and began sucking Sam's juices off it. She could see from the way that his scrotum had contracted that he was about to come. Moments before he did her own orgasm started and she kept up the frantic rubbing so that another overlapped the first.

Feeling herself go weak, Sam closed the door and sat on the bathroom floor, trying to make sense of what was happening, wondering where her involvement with the mysterious Mr McLeod would lead her next.

Chapter Nine

SAM STOOD OUTSIDE the theatre on Shaftesbury Avenue waiting for Judy. She moved slightly away from the entrance as she didn't want anybody to think that she was going to see the Dreamboats, which indeed she was. She knew that this was actually a ridiculous worry. The anonymity of the city was something she cherished. No-one took any notice of anyone else. Everyone who passed her seemed to be on a mission with their heads down and shoulders braced, determined to get to where they were going in the fastest possible time.

Judy, back from New York, had had to work hard to persuade her to come to the show. She reasoned that Sam needed cheering up, and what better way to do it than go out and laugh at some men for the evening?

The hoarding at the front of the theatre showed pictures of six semi-naked men, in poses that women were presumably supposed to find sexy, although from Sam's experience, most women would would find them laughable. They had every conceivable style of hair, from skinhead to waist-length curly perm, obviously trying to cover every type of taste in coiffure. It also seemed they had taken to heart the old adage that every woman loved a man in uniform, or at least half in uniform. To say that the Dreamboats used sexual stereotyping was an understatement, thought Sam, as she studied the photographs of them flexing their well-oiled muscles.

She watched as groups of women swarmed past her into the theatre and felt slightly disdainful. However, overhearing snatches of their conversation, she soon realised that none of them was there expecting to be turned on, but rather they were out for a laugh with the girls. Exactly like Judy and her. She wondered if it was at all possible for men to be seen purely as sex objects. Could the tables be turned so simply? Before she could think any more on the subject Judy was by her side.

'Hi. I've been wondering all day if I can stand being driven wild by six men stripping off for me,' said Judy, making a face that suggested the exact opposite was going to happen.

'I wouldn't worry about your blood pressure too much,' replied Sam, nodding at the billboard. 'They look too plasticky for me. I'm sure the one on the end was in *Thunderbirds*.'

Judy studied the poster. 'Well, at least it's another blow for sexual equality.'

'I was just thinking about that. I'm not sure if it's so easy to objectify men.'

'I didn't mean that,' laughed Judy, squinting at the photographs of the Dreamboats. 'I mean that it's nice to know that some men finally understand the pain of having your legs waxed.'

The atmosphere inside the foyer was like the end of term party at a girls' boarding school. Many women in their thirties and older were squealing like teenagers. It seemed that the idea of men stripping off in front of them had sent them hurtling back into adolescence, but perhaps that was the best spirit to see the show in. Sam noticed that a lot of groups seemed to be on hen nights, something she felt she was never going to experience with her luck in men.

It was no quieter once Sam and Judy found their seats inside. 'I don't think I've ever been with so many women in my life,' said Sam.

'I know. All that oestrogen. Do you think that by the end of the show all our periods will be in sync?'

Sam burst out laughing just as the lights went down and a hush settled on the auditorium. From the loud speakers a voice boomed over a roll of drums, 'Ladies, the Empire is proud to present . . . the Dreamboats.' The crowd went berserk and it seemed that only Sam and Judy remained seated. Music started playing and the curtain rose to reveal six men in white navy uniforms, the jackets undone.

'It's *HMS Pinafore* dress,' screamed Judy.

The Dreamboats danced in formation whilst stripping off. There were hundreds of catcalls to get them off and the men soon obliged. Down to their tiny G-strings, they rubbed baby oil into their bodies and then picked women from the audience who were only too eager to help rub in some more.

Judy hadn't stopped laughing since the show began. 'If you can't beat 'em, join 'em. Get 'em off,' she shouted towards the stage.

Sam looked at her friend in amazement. Then

she realised that Judy was right and she might just as well enter the spirit of the show. 'We want to see more – now,' she screamed, jumping up and down in her seat.

The men kept their G-strings on and instead simulated sex on top of the women brave enough to get up on the stage. These women were helpless with laughter. Sam thought how different it would be if it were women strippers lying over men. There would be no laughter.

After several more themed routines – motorcycle cops, construction workers, Vikings – which never went further than the G-strings, Sam and Judy decided they'd seen enough.

'I thought that Village People had split up,' said Sam as they left the theatre.

Needing a drink, they headed around the corner into Soho. They both commented on the strange split that had happened in the area, with trendy bars springing up between the sleazy, exploitative sex joints. They sat outside one of the cafés with a bottle of wine and people-watched.

'Look at him in the mac,' said Judy, not attempting to hide who she was pointing at, 'he's definitely on his way to a Nude Bed Show.'

'Nobody could accuse you of judging a book by its cover, could they, Jude?'

'Oh, come on, Sam, men are obvious at the best of times.'

Sure enough, the man looked around nervously and then disappeared through one of the red-lit doorways.

'Sometimes I think the gulf between men and women is impossible. There'll never be any real understanding. We just operate in completely different ways,' Sam commented.

'You're getting a bit deep, aren't you?' Judy replied, taking the mickey.

Sam glared at her friend. 'Take tonight. If that had been women performing and a male audience it would have been serious, not a laughing matter. Also it would have been sexual, erotic. To the men, anyway.'

'Where's this conversation going, Germaine?'

'I don't know. I've just been thinking about women's sexuality and what really turns them on.'

'And?' asked Judy, almost impatiently.

'I think, for many, it's scenarios that can't be translated into real life. Like a rape fantasy – it's not really rape, is it? It's having a tall, dark, handsome stranger take you forcefully but really with your permission.'

Judy thought for a while. 'I guess you're right. My pet theory is that the more confident and more powerful the woman is, the more her fantasies will include being submissive, dominated and humiliated.'

'What, to balance things up?'

'I suppose so.'

'I think you've got a point there,' said Sam, deep in thought.

The next day Marcus rang in the afternoon. 'Recovered from Las Vegas?'

'Just about,' Sam replied, sleepily.

For the rest of their stay in Las Vegas neither of them had referred to what happened that night. The remainder of the holiday had passed quickly and uneventfully, and Sam felt glad to be back in London.

166

'Good,' said Marcus. 'So are you up for going out tonight? Just somewhere casual, no need to dress up.'

Still half asleep, Sam took down the address of a pub, only realising after she had put the phone down that it was in a rough part of the East End. Whatever was Marcus up to, meeting in a pub in that area?

She took him at his word that evening, dressing in just jeans and a man's white cotton shirt. A few minutes before her taxi was due there was a knock on her door.

'Miss Winterton?' asked a spotty-faced teenager.

'Yes.'

'It's from Mr McLeod.'

The boy handed her a suitcase and fled. As with the trunk before, there was an envelope attached to the side. She took the case into her hallway and shook it. Although the suitcase was quite large it was fairly light and she could hear something hard banging around inside. She ripped open the envelope to find a note in Marcus's familiar looped handwriting.

Dear Sam, Please bring this with you to the pub. It's locked. Frustrating, I know, but worth the wait. See you at eight. M.

Sam tried the locks just in case. Why did Marcus always have to make such a drama out of things? Then she smiled. Marcus knew how to set the scene. He knew that creating great tension led to some great climaxes.

As she travelled in the taxi, she racked her brains trying to guess what was in the case. She knew that there were likely to be clothes, but for what? The taxi slowed down and Sam gazed out of the window. The view was depressing. Most of the houses in the street had been boarded up against squatters and practically all of the street lamps were out. There was no-one on the street and they passed a dirty all-night grocer's where a forlorn shopkeeper sat miserably waiting for custom.

'There's the Royal Oak, love, at the end of that alley,' said the driver, pointing. 'Are you sure that's where you're meant to be going? I wouldn't let any lady I knew go to The Royal Oak on her own.'

Sam bridled at his casual sexism but realised he was genuinely concerned. She assumed a brisk, confident manner, something she didn't feel inside. 'I'm meeting someone there. I'm sure it'll be fine.'

'If you say so, love,' said the cabbie as Sam handed over her fare.

Unbelievably, the road was still cobbled. She knew that conservationists actually argued for the preservation of cobbled streets but in this instance it only served to add to the general air of almost Dickensian squalor. She ducked into the alleyway, alarmed at being on her own in such a place. Why would Marcus frequent a pub in this area? As she opened the door of the pub she prayed that he would already be there waiting for her.

The smell of cigarette smoke and stale beer was overwhelming, as was the noise coming from the twenty to thirty men standing around drinking, shouting over and above the already too loud tinny music. Sam looked around desperately for

Marcus and at first she couldn't see him. Then she did a double take as she realised that the man playing pool in the corner in a pair of old jeans and a lumberjack shirt was indeed the millionaire businessman. Sam's heart skipped a beat. She liked this Marcus, the working-class hero, the bit of rough trade.

She fought her way through the crowd, attracting hostile looks as she banged people's legs with the case.

'Marcus, help me,' she shouted, once she was near enough.

He looked up, smiled and took his shot on the black ball. Sam waited impatiently for the game to finish.

'Don't bother to rush,' she said, as he finally came over and picked up the case.

'I had money riding on that shot. You wouldn't want me to lose, would you?' he asked with a twinkle in his eye.

Sam looked heavenward. 'God forbid that should happen. Now, are you going to tell me why we're in this hell hole?'

'I thought you were open to all new experiences.'

For one horrible minute, Sam wondered if Marcus had plans for her and the whole pub but looking around it became obvious that none of the men knew about her or was particularly interested. Their attention seemed to be focused on the other side of the room.

'What's going on over there?' she asked Marcus.

'Go and have a look. I'll get you a pint.'

Sam edged her way through the men, attracting

more dirty looks. Finally, managing to get to the front of the gathered crowd, she saw what was grabbing their attention. On a small stage lay a woman in her early forties performing a desultory striptease. Both the woman and her act had obviously seen better days. Her make-up was plastered on in a desperate attempt, Sam guessed, to hide the signs of ageing. Her bright blue eye shadow was smudged and her red lipstick, of a shade even Judy would pale at, had bled, causing lots of scarlet vein-like lines around her mouth. Beside her on the stage lay a red satin mini skirt and a red feather boa. The other boa on the stage was real: the main focus of her act was a large snake writhing between her thighs and coiling its way up her body. The snake appeared to be shedding its skin, adding to the sorry nature of the whole enterprise.

Wearily, the stripper struggled out of a limp black bra and threw it at the crowd. A jeer went up.

'I hope you've washed that snake,' shouted one man.

'I bet the snake hopes the same thing about her,' added another.

Sam shuddered at the callousness of the audience. It seemed so different from the good-natured catcalling at the Dreamboats' show. As the woman added her knickers to the pile of clothes on the stage, Sam turned and walked away. Apart from the stripper and a young, tarty blonde barmaid, Sam was the only other woman in the place. What on earth was Marcus doing bringing her here?

Marcus had finished his game and was waiting

by the pool table for her. 'What did you think of Flo?' he asked.

'It's not quite the Moulin Rouge, is it?'

Marcus laughed. 'She's been doing that act for years. She never gets any better but I hear that a couple of the snakes have gone on to bigger things.'

'Marcus, that's cruel,' she said, looking suspiciously at the murky pint of beer that he held out for her.

'Go on, drink it,' he said. 'It's fine. I don't think they get much call for white wine spritzers in here.'

Sam just looked at him, trying to fathom out what was going on. From the noise coming from the crowd Sam guessed that Flo had come to the climax of her act, though she dreaded to think what that climax was.

'By the way, this is Richard,' said Marcus, nodding towards a thin, nondescript-looking man in his mid-thirties. 'He's the Oak's best pool player and I want you to play against him. Not quite a bet, but I'll give you five thousand if you win. As I remember, you're quite a hot player.'

'I haven't played for years and you know I'm no match for him,' she said, smiling at Richard, who was pretending to ignore their conversation. 'I presume the forfeit has something to do with the case?'

'Let's just play, shall we?' replied Marcus.

He soon had the balls set up and was flipping a coin to see who would break. Sam won the toss. She took a big sip of beer, then got into position. She carefully lined up the cue and struck the white ball with a hard, clean hit. Four balls went into the pockets, three of them stripes. She aimed for the next striped ball and it too dropped into a pocket with a satisfying clink. The following shot was tricky and she had to put a spin on the white. The stripe bounced off the cushion and narrowly missed the pocket but Sam was still pleased with the head start she had given herself.

Richard walked over to the table. From the calluses on his hands, Sam guessed he was a blue collar worker. She compared him to Marcus and the difference between the two men's diet, lifestyle and wealth was obvious. However, Marcus and Richard seemed to get on well.

What Sam couldn't take away from Richard was his exceptional pool playing. Her opening triumph was soon dashed as Richard put down one ball after another until he was on the black. Casually he potted that too, looking pleased with himself.

'You wanna make that best of three?' he asked.

'No. I give in,' said Sam. 'I'm not in your league.' She turned to Marcus. 'I take it that there's a forfeit?'

She half expected him to say she was to sleep with Richard, which was not a prospect that turned her on. Instead, Marcus gave her the key for the case and told her to go to the ladies' and open it.

The toilet was damp and cold. The old, nicotine-stained wallpaper was peeling off, the toilet seat was missing and the tap in the sink wouldn't turn off. There was hardly any room to turn around and Sam had difficulty in opening the case. When she finally succeeded she stood still for a moment, coming to terms with what was inside and getting an inkling of what her forfeit was.

The first item in the suitcase was a cheap red satin dress very similar to the skirt Flo had discarded. On it was another of Marcus's notes:

As professional as she was, Flo was only the support act. Heading the bill tonight at the Royal Oak is a lovely young woman new to the business. Please get dressed and on stage as soon as possible. I know I can rely on you to bring the house down. M.

Sam rifled through the case with horror. Aside from the usual stripper's gear Marcus had included a variety of vibrators and dildos in different colours and sizes, some so big, the very thought of them made her wince. Among them was the dildo that he had used on her in Las Vegas. She made a connection. She wondered if this was a punishment and Marcus was making her pay for his inability to perform. Maybe he wanted her to degrade herself. He'd certainly picked the right environment for her to do it.

But that just wasn't Marcus. He wasn't vengeful and Sam seriously believed he meant it when he said that he loved her. She decided that he seriously wanted her to enjoy this forfeit. The thought of going out in front of those men terrified her but she knew that Marcus would never do anything to put her at risk. She blanked everything out of her mind and got changed.

For a second, when she looked at herself in the chipped mirror above the sink, she almost didn't recognise herself. The clothes certainly did the trick of transforming her into a cheap stripper and the make-up Marcus had provided, a mixture of lurid green eye-shadows and Flo-red lipsticks, finished off the job. The cold made her nipples poke through the thin material of the dress. Lifting the hem she straightened her suspenders and last of all put on the black stiletto shoes. As she did so, Flo walked into the toilet, still naked. She looked at Sam appraisingly.

'You'll do fine, girl,' she said in a raspy voice. 'You give 'em hell, darling.'

Sam thanked her, feeling a strange sense of camaraderie with the battle weary old stripper. As she squeezed past Flo to get out, she was sure that she felt the snake lick her arm.

She carried the case back to Marcus, the height of her shoes making her hips swagger. Marcus noticed straight away. 'It looks like you've got the hang of it already,' he said. 'Keep that movement up and you'll have everyone going.'

'Is that all I have to do, Marcus?' she asked in a teasing voice.

'No. I paid a lot of money for all those sex toys and I want to see them fully used. Okay?'

'Anything you say, boss.'

Sam acted coolly, as if stripping off and fucking herself with dildos in front of a room of strangers was an everyday event. But her insides were churning and she felt sick with fear. She asked Marcus to go and get her another drink and he returned with a large vodka.

'I'm scared,' she said, knocking the vodka back in one.

'You're completely safe,' he assured her. 'And admit it. Doesn't the prospect of undressing in front of all those men excite you as well?'

Sam had to admit that it did. She was aware that Marcus knew that the more she debased herself in front of this crowd, the wetter she would get.

The music on the jukebox was turned off as the landlord of the pub climbed up on the stage.

'Gentlemen and gentlemen, it gives me great pleasure to present a new, young act never seen in the East End before. Please give a big round of applause for Samantha.'

There was some sporadic clapping and Sam turned to Marcus, horrified. 'I'm going to fall flat on my face. Literally.'

Marcus smiled reassuringly and gave her a shove in the direction of the stage.

This time the men made way for Sam as she moved forward. She could hear appreciative comments about her looks, dress and figure. Perhaps they would be easy to please after all, especially as her only competition was Flo.

The familiar brassy sound of 'The Stripper' burst from the pub's speakers. Sam climbed on to the stage and for a moment she just stood there. In all the time she had been getting ready she hadn't actually thought of how she would strip. She could feel the crowd getting restless so she pulled herself together and scoured the audience. She picked one attractive man and decided she would concentrate on him, trying to blot out everything else that was around her.

She began to sway her hips from side to side and the man cheered appreciatively. She then lifted her arms into the air, bringing them down slowly and on to her breasts. Keeping the same pace she slid the straps of her dress down over her arms and then allowed the cheap satin material to fall to the floor.

There were wolf-whistles from all around the room. From that moment she knew that she had them all on her side. She felt a surge of confidence mingled with a rush of sexual excitement. Turning her back on the audience, she bent over and wiggled her buttocks at them, knowing they could see the outline of her vagina. There was another collective cheer. While she was turned away from the men Sam undid her bra at the back, whirling around to tear it off. She shook her breasts at them and they roared.

That was it, there was no holding her back. In the spirit of the moment she grabbed one of the men at the front and dragged him up on to the stage. She pushed his head into her cleavage. The man responded by grabbing hold of her breasts and pushing a nipple into his mouth. It felt good to her but laughing, she shouldered him off the stage and back into the crowd.

The landlord had placed Sam's case on the stage. Sitting on the edge of it, she took off her shoes. Then, stretching one leg out at a time, she tantalisingly rolled down her stockings and threw them into the audience. With her legs bare, she stepped back into her shoes again and whipped off her suspender belt. She stood at the front of the stage, legs apart, practically thrusting her crotch into the faces of the men in the front row. She knew that they were dying to see her naked, to see the source of the damp patch that had appeared between her legs.

She was aware that more and more of the men were getting erections from looking at her. Some had even started to rub their groins through their trousers and Sam returned the compliment, running her fingers over the wet material that covered her own sex. This drove the crowd wild so she sat back down on the case, opened her legs wide and yanked her pants to one side for a few seconds to let them look at her lips. There were lustful groans all around the room.

Sam rubbed her swollen labia then fingered herself. She was soaking now, and desperate to use one of the sex toys. In one smooth move she had her knickers off. Totally brazen now, she walked to the front of the stage, turned around and bent over. With her hands, she parted her buttocks so everyone could have a good long look at her spread labia, glistening under the spotlight.

Through her legs she could see that a number of the men had taken their cocks out and were openly wanking. She walked over to the case and selected a six-inch gold vibrator. She intended to start small and work her way up. Resting her head against the case, she lay on the stage with her legs wide open facing the audience. The men moved closer, craning their necks to get a better look.

Since Marcus had shaved her she had let her hair grow back, in the hope that he would do it again. For a moment she wished she was bare now so that the audience could see every centimetre of her sex – the way her clitoris bulged and the full beauty of the folds of her labia. But from their obvious delight at the way she teased them, twisting strands of her pubic hair around her fingers, she guessed that they didn't mind a bit.

She turned on the vibrator and the men were silent so they could hear the faint buzz. With the head of it she played around her vulva, enjoying not only the sensation it was giving her but also the pleasure it was giving the men watching her do it. She began fucking herself, slowly, all the time making sure that the men could see everything she was doing. She took most of the vibrator into herself and for a while just lay back, playing with her nipples while the sex toy vibrated her insides.

Out of the corner of her eye, she could see Marcus. He, too, had his cock out but he wasn't masturbating like the others. He had the blonde barmaid kneeling in front of him as he shoved his cock in and out of her mouth. He saw Sam looking and winked. As she marvelled at the stiffness of his penis, for a moment she felt a familiar pang of jealousy, remembering how soft it was when she had sucked it in Las Vegas.

'Go on, fuck yourself,' shouted a lust-filled voice from the crowd and Sam's attention returned to what she was doing.

The gold vibrator had loosened her up and her labia now spread of their own accord. Taking the vibrator out, she opened the case and selected a ten-inch black dildo. Closing the suitcase again, she bent forward over it and plunged the dildo deep inside her. There were whoops of encouragement and several of the men came, unable to hold back any more. But Sam wasn't finished with them yet.

Again she lay on the stage, this time lifting her legs high into the air so that her anus was on view as fully as her sex. Once again she turned on the gold vibrator and slowly inserted it into her anus. The man who had licked her nipples earlier lost complete control and she could feel drops of his come hit her as he ejaculated high in the air.

Sam called another man from the front to come up and assist her. Under her instruction, he fucked her with the vibrator while manically pumping his stiff rod. 'Any more volunteers?' she called out lewdly.

A man shot up on to the stage and she made him select another dildo from the case. This one was almost as wide as it was long and she gasped as he rammed it deep into her vagina.

'Fuck me, fuck me,' she screamed and the man did as he was told, at the same time shunting his foreskin back and forth.

Catching Richard's eye, Sam motioned him to come over. He obeyed, his penis hard but still hidden in his trousers.

'Take your cock out,' she commanded.

Undoing his flies, he revealed the biggest dick Sam had ever seen. She was mesmerised and wanted it in her mouth, though she doubted she could take more than a quarter of it. Richard obliged and as her lips stretched wide to accommodate the massive head, she could see the barmaid, similarly struggling on Marcus's engorged cock.

'Oh suck it, suck it,' moaned Richard, as he thrust his hips, ramming more of this monster into Sam's throat.

She could tell that the crowd was about to explode. Those men who hadn't come were almost beside themselves with desire while those who had were erect again and ready to shoot. With every orifice being filled, Sam too desperately wanted to have an orgasm. Unwilling to let

Richard's penis out of her mouth even for a second she put her arm out and motioned for everyone to come closer. As they did so she began to massage her clitoris. She rubbed harder and faster and the two men working on her body matched her speed. Richard also shoved more of his cock into her mouth until she thought she would choke.

It was obvious Sam had begun to come. Her body twitched and writhed in ecstasy and her screams, although muffled by Richard's cock, were the sign for everyone else to let go too. Her mouth was flooded with Richard's come and the two men at her crotch spurted over her stomach and breasts. The row of the crowd coming as one was almost deafening and come rained down on her from every direction. Eventually the pub grew silent. Sam propped herself up and looked over at Marcus to see the barmaid proudly wiping his come from her chin.

Chapter Ten

THE LIGHTS FLASHING in time with the music made Sam's head throb even more. It had been a mistake to come, she thought, looking around her. She was fed up with being jostled in the relentless toing and froing of the crowd. As per usual it had been Judy's idea, but the place only confirmed Sam's suspicions about West End clubs that attracted soap stars and those who thought it glamorous to stand next to them. If one more ex-footballer wearing too much gold jewellery made a pass at her she'd scream.

She strained her eyes trying to see through the thick swirls of dry ice to Judy, who was somewhere at the bar. It looked as if she was talking to two men. As neither of them looked like Gazza she guessed that it must be Alan and his friend, Danny. She squinted, trying to get a better look, but a new whoosh of smoke completely obscured her view. She was then distracted by having to fend off a man with a bad perm whose opening line was the priceless, 'You know, it's a myth about footballers not being able to shag the night before a game.'

In her infinite wisdom, Judy had decided that Sam needed a date and had fixed her up with Alan's friend. Sam hated blind dates and had protested, but to no avail. Once Judy had decided on something, especially if she thought it was for your own good, that was it. Sam had been dreading this evening. Judy's taste in men erred a little on the loud, macho side and Sam guessed that she would be spending the evening with some rugger bugger type trying to interest her in an arm-wrestling match. Their choice of venue for the evening didn't bode well either.

Judy's smiling face appeared through the smoke.

'Sam, this is Alan and this, is Danny.'

Inwardly, Sam breathed a sigh of relief. He was passable, to say the least, which was probably why Judy looked relieved, too. Not until they arrived at the club had Judy confessed that she'd never actually met Danny before. Her assurance had been that Alan had said he was good-looking. Sam had had her doubts as to Alan's judgment, as she invariably found that what men deemed handsome in other men was very different to what a woman would think.

The more Sam gazed at Danny the better he looked, although he wasn't the type she usually went for. He was pretty rather than handsome, almost feminine. Straight away she noticed his big grey eyes with eyelashes a woman would die for and his full and sensual mouth. He looked as if he were in his early thirties but could have been older. His accent placed him from somewhere in the south west of England. Danny said hello in a gentle, lilting voice and Sam felt her headache disappearing.

He shook her hand and she could tell from his expression that he was also pleased with how she looked.

'Great to meet you,' he said, as he sat down next to her.

Sam wondered what to say next. This was what she hated most about this kind of thing. Even if you made it past the first hurdle and the man wasn't Quasimodo, you then had to develop a false conversation where each of you gave the other your potted history in five minutes, while both pretended that it was a huge coincidence that you should meet like this. Luckily, Danny took the matter into his own hands.

'Sam, let's just put our cards on the table.' He said this loud enough for Judy to hear and Sam could tell she was listening. 'We know that Judy here kindly thinks we are such desperately sad and lonely people that she has to set us up on a date, so let's not disappoint her. Do you want to dance?'

Sam could see that Judy was just about to interrupt. 'Well, we all know what a busybody Judy is, don't we, and yes, I'd love to have a dance,' she said as she stood and playfully poked her tongue out at her friend.

She was gratified to see that Danny could dance. Men who could dance had instant sex appeal but unfortunately, they were few and far between. The music changed gear and slowed down. Sam stood still for a few seconds, unsure of what to do. Once again, Danny took charge, putting his hands in the air as if ready to waltz.

'May I have this dance?'

'Certainly, sir.'

At first Danny danced a parody of a waltz, making Sam giggle. Then his face became serious and he held her close to his chest.

'I'm really glad Judy introduced us.'

'So am I,' replied Sam, laughing again. 'To be honest Judy's arranged a couple of blind dates in the past and they were complete nightmares.'

'I take it I'm not too scary then,' said Danny.

When they returned to the table it was clear that Judy and Alan weren't really interested in holding any conversation. They were entwined in each other's arms, passionately kissing.

'It shouldn't be allowed in public,' said Danny.

Sam was surprised to see that his face was deadly serious until he couldn't control himself any longer and broke out laughing. His laugh had a deep resonance. She found herself laughing along with him as they turned their backs on the happy couple and walked towards the bar.

They began telling each other their respective histories, but there wasn't any embarrassment – both genuinely wanted to know about the other. Sam steered clear of talking about work. She guessed that Danny was something in finance but the fact that she didn't have a job bothered her. Danny seemed to sense that she didn't want to talk about it and also avoided the subject.

She found herself wondering what he would be like in bed. She could tell that underneath his jeans and T-shirt he was slim but lithe. She smiled to herself when she wondered what his cock would look like. She was just thinking about his balls when Danny asked her if she would like to

184

go for something to eat.

'Uh, aah, yes, that would be lovely,' she stammered.

'Good. There's a great Italian place just around the corner.'

They went over to say their goodbyes to Judy and Alan and the couple managed to separate themselves just long enough for Judy to give Sam a knowing wink which Sam studiously ignored.

'I'll speak to you tomorrow,' said Sam.

Judy barely heard her as Alan lunged at her neck and playfully bit her.

At the restaurant their conversation took a more intimate turn. Danny revealed that up until a year ago he had been married and the break-up had led to nine months of celibacy. Sam quickly got the message that this period was definitely over. She found herself telling him about Toby. Danny was sympathetic but Sam felt that in someway she was betraying Toby. She was beginning to accept that he had given up on her but she still couldn't bring herself to give up on him. The strong desire that she felt for Danny confused her.

'So here I am – my lover has walked out on me, I've got no job and if it wasn't for selling off some shares, I'd be defaulting on my mortgage.' Sam hated the way she sounded so pathetic. 'I don't suppose you've got a job going, have you?'

'Not unless you've just written a book. I'm in publishing,' said Danny, then added, 'However, I have got a vacancy for a lover.'

Sam was silent, uncertain how to respond.

Danny continued. 'I'd really like to stay with you tonight.'

Sam thought briefly about playing hard to get but decided it was an artifice that Danny would see through.

'I'd love you to, as well,' she said, taking one step further away from Toby.

In the taxi they kissed for the first time. Sam was very aware of how different Danny's lips felt to those of the many men she had kissed before. They weren't hard; they seemed to melt into hers. He kissed her gently, almost apprehensively, as if he thought she would stop him.

Sam waited for a hand to move to her breasts, but while one arm was around her shoulders the other lay limply in his lap. It seemed as if he needed her to lead. Again, this was so different from her other lovers. It suited Sam fine. She didn't want to be with somebody who reminded her of what had gone before. She picked up his hand and placed it on her breast. Danny responded at once, kneaded and massaging through her blouse but not daring to slip his hand under the material.

Arriving back home, Sam began to relish her dominant position. They were barely through her front door when she ordered him to take off his clothes. Danny looked unsure what to do and just stood there.

'Do as you're told and take your clothes off.'

He smiled sheepishly at Sam and took off his T-shirt. His chest was brown as if he had been on a recent holiday and on his shoulder there was an intricate tattoo of a pouncing tiger. Sam watched him for a moment then left him to finish undressing and went to her bedroom.

Opening her underwear drawer she rooted

around until she found her black basque and black stockings. She quickly changed, and put on a pair of black stilettos, admiring her image in the mirror. To top off her dominatrix look she reached into her drawer again, finding two filmy black silk scarves. She intended to make Danny completely submissive. She spent several minutes fine-touching her look then strode back into the living room to find Danny still in his boxer shorts helping himself to a drink.

'I told you to undress, didn't I?'

Danny turned around and nearly dropped his drink at the sight of her. She knew she looked stunning. She had scraped her hair back into a severe bun and painted her lips a dark purple colour which made her look stern and forbidding. In her heels she was taller than him and there was no getting away from the fact that her body looked great in the basque. Her breasts were pushed up, faking a magnificent cleavage, and her waist was slightly constricted. Knickerless, the triangle of her pubic hair was framed by her suspenders and the lacy trim at the bottom of the basque.

As a finishing touch she had located her riding crop and was brandishing it menacingly. Toby had bought it for her when they had gone horse riding together but Sam had been pretty sure that he hadn't intended for it to be used on a horse. Unfortunately, Toby hadn't stayed around long enough for her to find out.

Danny recovered his composure and did as he was told. From the way his penis stood to attention, Sam could tell he was comfortable with the role he'd been assigned. His cock was slim but long and the same deep olive colour as the rest of his body. As Sam moved towards him she could see it twitching with excitement. She remembered the Pain scenario and ordered Danny to his knees. She thrust her groin into his face so that her pubic hair tickled the end of his nose.

'Lick me.'

Danny was only too happy to serve. His tongue darted out and immediately found the opening of her sex. He leaned forward slightly so he could probe all the way in with his tongue. He seized Sam's hips, partly to balance himself and partly to bring her further on to his searching tongue. Sam felt her juices mix with Danny's saliva and seep down her thighs. She looked down and watched as his tongue parted her labia.

His licking became more insistent as he moved his tongue on to her clitoris and slid two fingers into her vagina, the muscles under his tattoo rippling from the effort. Sam grabbed his hair and buried the whole of his face in her groin. The noisy slurping sound he made only served to make her even wetter.

Highly aroused, Sam was in danger of losing control of the situation. She forcefully pushed Danny away and ordered him into the bedroom. He complied without a sound and lay on the bed, waiting for her next move. She produced the two silk scarves and expertly tied Danny's arms to the bedposts. As Toby had pointed out when they had bought the bed, they were ideal for that particular use. From the flicker of worry on Danny's face, Sam guessed that he had never had a woman do this to him before and was wondering if he really was safe. She was pleased with this effect. A bit of fear was all part of the game.

She picked up a candlestick from her bedside table and lit the candle, holding it over Danny's chest. Slowly she tipped it, letting the hot wax drip on to his chest. Danny's face registered pain but his cock registered pleasure as it stiffened noticeably. There was no doubt in Sam's mind that he was enjoying every minute of this torture.

She put down the candle, having thought about her next move, savouring her dominant role. Danny went to say something but Sam made it clear that only she was allowed to speak.

'Spread your legs and lift your hips,' she said, placing a pillow under his behind.

She leaned forward, prizing his thighs even further apart with her hands as her face came closer and closer to his balls. She prodded each with her tongue, and then sucked one into her mouth, making Danny yelp. She ignored him and repeated the move on his other ball. Then with her hand she lifted his scrotum out of the way and let her tongue trace a line all the way down his perineum towards his anus, where she licked around his secret opening.

Danny cried out and Sam warned him to lie still and be quiet or else she would stop. He acquiesced immediately. She began licking at his anus again, this time allowing her tongue to probe just inside the tight hole. She could tell that Danny was struggling to keep quiet and she gently squeezed his balls as a further warning. His balls felt heavy with sperm and Sam knew that she would have to hold back for a moment or he would explode.

'Please,' begged Danny.

Sam reared up and slapped him across the face, silencing him.

She reached over and opened her drawer full of sex toys, getting out a small white vibrator. She then stood up so her vagina was in alignment with Danny's face. Slightly bending her knees, she sucked the vibrator into her vulva, quickly building up speed and rhythm. Danny's eyes were bright with desire, intently watching every move she made.

'I'd bet you wish this was your cock, don't you, Danny? How desperate are you to fuck me?'

Danny could hardly speak. 'You know how much I want it.'

Sam rubbed her clitoris as she pumped the vibrator in and out and she could feel the tingly sensations of the beginning of an orgasm. She was tempted to allow herself to come but decided against it – she had work to do.

Taking the vibrator out of her vagina, she knelt down in front of Danny again. His legs were still wide apart. Sam eyed his anus, which glistened from her saliva, then assaulted Danny's virgin hole with the vibrator, her juices making the perfect lubricant. Danny winced as his anus stretched to accommodate this intruder. But as most of the vibrator disappeared inside him he began to respond, squirming with delight at this new sensation. Sam gently fucked him until she sensed he was on the brink of orgasm. Then she stopped abruptly, leaving the vibrator inside him.

'Please don't stop,' pleaded Danny, breathlessly.

Sam raised her hand as if to hit him again. 'I'm warning you.'

She revelled in this new role. She enjoyed taking Danny to the brink and then refusing him his pleasure. But she wasn't sure how long it could last. She too had to be satisfied. Her need to have an orgasm was also becoming overwhelming.

Quickly she straddled him and sat on his cock. Danny let out a long, blissful moan as she reached behind herself and started to fuck him with the vibrator while gyrating her hips to satiate her own needs on his throbbing cock. Danny was no longer able to keep quiet and let out a stream of oaths as the vibrator ploughed into his anus. Sam could no long control him. Indeed she could no longer control herself as his long cock moved about inside her, her clitoris stimulated each time she rubbed against his stomach.

She knew that she could come at any time so started to move herself and the vibrator faster. As her orgasm began she could feel her muscles contract around Danny's cock, which proved too much for him. He screamed as his orgasm exploded and his come spurted into her, filling her up. The torrent of his juices seemed to go on forever.

Later, Danny confessed with a sincerity that Sam took as genuine, that it was the best fuck he'd ever had in his life. Sam, unsure how to play it now that the sex was over, smiled weakly. But the smile never reached her eyes. Sexually it had been great – she had enjoyed exploring this new part of her sensuality. But she couldn't disguise the fact that, however nice Danny was, deep down she would rather have been in bed with the man she loved. She lay down next to Danny and held on to him, closing her eyes and trying unsuccessfully to imagine that it was Toby lying beside her.

The next morning Sam awoke to find Danny gone and a note on his pillow, saying sorry he had to leave but he had a business meeting. He had left his phone number and asked her to get in touch with him. As she stretched her arms high above her head, she realised that she would never see him again. As nice as he was, it was purely a one-night stand.

The phone rang and she leapt out of bed to answer it. As she had suspected, it was Marcus.

'You should become a professional,' he said. 'Your act was out of this world.'

For a second, Sam thought he was talking about the night with Danny then realised he was referring to her strip act in the pub. 'Are you ringing up for a repeat performance?'

'Not quite, but I would like to see you tonight as I've arranged a game of poker with a very old friend from Egypt. You'll like him a lot.'

'Is he good? Will we win?' asked Sam, not really relishing another forfeit so soon after Danny. Besides, her bank balance needed some attention.

'Possibly. So I'll see you at seven.'

As usual Marcus hung up before Sam could argue with him. She wondered who this friend was and whether she would like him, although liking a man when fucking them had not been on her list of priorities.

Getting ready that evening, Sam thought she should perhaps dress on the conservative side.

From the tone of Marcus's voice she had gathered that this friend was an important person. Her looking like a cheap tart might not do Marcus any favours, however much he might personally like that look. With this in mind she chose a navy blue linen skirt and jacket and prim white silk blouse, done up to the top button. The blue shoes she chose were of a sensible height and she wore her hair in a chignon. To complete her virginal image, she wore pristine white cotton underwear.

As usual Marcus rang up from his car when he arrived outside her flat. Sam took one more look at herself and laughed out loud at the difference in how she looked from the last time he had seen her.

In the car Marcus was similarly amused. 'You look as if you're on your way to a Conservative Party branch meeting.'

'I just felt like a change of image. I look okay, don't I?' she asked, insecurity showing in her voice.

'You look as lovely as ever, just a bit different from how I've seen you looking lately,' he said, grinning.

She looked him over in turn and found that, as usual, he was immaculate in a grey suit, white shirt and dark red tie. She changed the subject. 'Where are we playing?' She knew better than to ask what the forfeit might be.

'At my friend's house. His name is Simon, an anglicisation, needless to say.'

The car was soon speeding through the streets of London, the pavements shimmering from the recent rain. Leaning back in the deep leather seat, Sam pressed the button to wind down the window and enjoyed the smell of the fresh summer rain. There was a companionable silence between Marcus and her. They were soon in Kensington, a venue far removed from the grime of the Royal Oak. Sam loved the way that Marcus seemed as comfortable in an area like this as he did in a rough East End pub. She looked up admiringly at the tall white houses flashing past. She would never be able to afford one of them, although the price would be a mere trifle to someone like Marcus.

The car stopped outside a house that was larger than any Sam had seen on the way. At the top of the six marble steps two gigantic pillars lined the entrance way leading to a large, stained-glass panelled door. Before they had a chance to ring the bell, the door was opened by a maid and without uttering a word she showed them in to the drawing room. Sam was glad their host wasn't there so she could have a nose around at how the other half lived. No matter how much time she spent with Marcus she still wasn't accustomed to the grandeur of other people's lives.

The room, lit by two chandeliers, was lined with thousands of beautifully bound books. Sam guessed that they were there more for their appearance than their content and she doubted that the owner had read even a fraction of them. One side of the room was taken up by an oval mahogany table that could comfortably sit twelve and the other side had three leather sofas which, from their immaculate appearance, Sam deduced were very rarely, if ever, used. Marcus sat down and beckoned her to join him.

Before Sam had a chance to voice her thoughts on the surrounding opulence, the door opened and in walked their host. Marcus jumped up and went over to Simon, pumping his hand and kissing each cheek. Sam stayed seated, waiting to be introduced. Simon looked to be in his late forties or early fifties, but well preserved. It was clear that he had spent a lot of his money on looking after himself. He had light green eyes and black hair without a speck of grey. His skin was a darker olive than Danny's and screwing her eyes up, Sam decided that, at a pinch, he could pass for Omar Sharif.

'Great to see you again,' said Marcus. 'This is Sam.'

'I've heard so much about you,' said Simon, as he took Sam's hand and kissed it.

Sam quelled the desire to ask exactly what he had heard. 'I'm pleased to meet you. You have a lovely house,' she said, formally.

Simon waved his hands expansively. 'It's nothing.'

Sam wondered what he thought something would be.

'Ah, my other guest,' said Simon, as the doorbell went again.

The maid showed in a man who had to be at least seventy. Sam gave Marcus a sharp look. He understood her meaning and shook his head. This man was not to be involved in any forfeit she might have to pay in the course of the evening.

'This is John Bart,' said Simon to Sam. 'A world class poker player. Now, what would everyone like to drink?'

Sam noted that Simon's Middle Eastern accent

had been subsumed beneath an Oxbridge pronunciation. He had undoubtedly spent many years in England. She wondered how he knew Marcus and, more importantly, how much he knew about their arrangement. So far, nothing he had said or done indicated that he knew anything.

The maid circulated with a tray of drinks and the four of them sat at one end of the large table, Sam sitting next to Simon, opposite Marcus and John. An unbroken pack of cards lay on the table top and Simon undid them and shuffled expertly. The men all looked deadly serious. Sam looked along the vast expanse of the table and felt there was something slightly ridiculous about the way they were all huddled together, but she knew better than to risk making a comment about it. John, especially, looked like a man for whom pleasure was no laughing matter. Since their first introduction he had said nothing. It was clear that he wasn't there to make small talk.

'How much are we starting with?' Simon directed the question solely at Marcus and John.

Sam gave him a look which he picked up on immediately.

'Forgive my manners,' he said, smiling at Sam. 'I'm not used to playing with ladies.' He gave her such a beseeching look that Sam forgave him instantly. She also felt fraudulent, as it wasn't up to her at all how much they played for.

Marcus decided they should start off with five thousand pounds each on the table. Sam was flabbergasted that even at a friendly game in someone's house the stakes should be so high. Simon agreed, stood up and went over to a magnificent Regency dresser. He opened a drawer and took out a bag of professional checkers.

'I'm sure I don't have to check that any of us are good for the money,' joked Simon, as he sat down and gave them each an equal share.

He cracked his knuckles and dealt them five cards each, his perfectly manicured fingers moving quickly and surely. Sam looked at her hand with dismay: she had nothing. Almost petulantly, she told them she was out. Marcus gave her a smile that implied there was plenty of time yet, which only made Sam think about what he had in mind for her.

On the next run Sam had almost a full house. She got rid of a jack of clubs and was amazed when her next card turned out to be the five of diamonds. Perfect. She put another hundred pounds on to the table, trying to read the minds of the others, knowing that poker was as much a game of bluff as skill. She sweated it out. Her hand was the last to be turned over. She had won.

Simon and Marcus looked genuinely pleased for her but John gave her a filthy look. He was not used to losing, especially to a woman. Sam, annoyed at John's ungentlemanly behaviour, decided that, if she was going to play, she was going to play to win. And for the next few games she did, much to everyone's surprise.

The room had become unbearably hot. Sam had removed her jacket and undone the top two buttons of her blouse. Similarly, the men had taken off their jackets and loosened their ties. All of them had been drinking non-stop and Sam was beginning to feel slightly woozy. She wasn't sure if it was the drink or not but she was convinced that she had seen a signal being sent between Marcus and Simon.

Ten minutes later, when she had won yet another game, she knew she had been right. Marcus, slightly slurring his words, suggested they spice up the game by playing strip poker. John looked even more shocked than Sam at this suggestion. It became clear that John was not in on Simon and Marcus's game but he said nothing and Sam detected a glint in his eyes.

'Great idea, don't you think? It is getting rather stuffy in here,' said Simon, in a tone that implied this was an everyday event.

Sam had mixed feelings. She was excited by the prospect of continuing her lucky streak and watching Marcus and Simon undress in front of her, though that meant John undressing too, perish the thought. But her time with Marcus had planted something of the devil in her, and she agreed.

On the next game John won and the other three paid their debt by forfeiting a shoe each. Sam was quite glad that John also won the next game and remained fully clothed while the three losers sacrificed another shoe. When Marcus produced four aces on the next hand the look of shock on John's face told her that he hadn't envisaged that he too might have to undress. Begrudgingly, and with some difficulty, he eased off one of his shoes while Simon quite happily whipped off his tie.

Sam realised that she would be showing more, quicker, than the others as she stood up to take off a stocking. The three men watched her intently as she lifted her skirt to undo her suspender. Simon asked her if she needed any help. She rebuffed him but allowed him to see the tops of her thighs. So much for dressing primly, she thought to herself.

The next game Sam won with a straight flush. She leaned back in her chair, ignoring Marcus removing his tie and John struggling out of his other shoe. Instead, she watched Simon take off his shirt. She was pleasantly surprised at how his body looked. For a man of his age everything seemed to be in working order. His torso was a darker shade of brown than his face and his muscles were still clearly defined. She admired the smattering of black hair on his chest, noting the occasional inevitable wisp of grey. Throwing the shirt on the floor, Simon turned and smiled at her.

'I hope you like what you see.'

Sam gave a subtle nod in agreement. When she looked across to Marcus, she could see that he wasn't looking happy with this turn of events. She was surprised, as she had assumed that if John, heaven forbid, wasn't the forfeit then Simon must be. Maybe Marcus didn't like it if she acted without his permission. He had promised her that their adventures together would be about exploring her sexuality but perhaps that wasn't true. She thought about their abortive attempt at sex together in Las Vegas. Again Sam had been active, taking a lead, demanding her pleasure, and he hadn't liked it. She had always been willing to give Marcus the benefit of the doubt, but maybe he was using her? She was going to put it to the test.

Sam lost the next few games. With sex on her

mind, she was no longer interested in winning. She wanted to reveal her body to Simon, to gauge his response. She was down to her bra and pants when she lost her fourth game in a row. Slowly she undid her bra and took it off. All eyes were on her. Marcus seethed. Sam glared at him. You don't control me, she thought. She turned her attention to Simon and was happy to note the outline of a very promising erection in his trousers.

Marcus and John still had most of their clothes on and most of the chips in front of them. It seemed to Sam that Simon had begun to throw his hands away, eager to lose his trousers, when Marcus turned over another winning hand. John then completely refused to take off any more clothes, muttering that the game was a travesty but noticeably not getting up to leave. But nobody cared. It was as if only Marcus, Simon and Sam were in the room.

It was a very odd situation. The prospect of winning meant nothing. Marcus seemed determined to lose in order that he might undress more quickly than Simon, thus forcing Sam's attention back on him. But Sam wanted to torment him and threw her cards on to the table.

'I'm not playing any more,' she said.

It was as much a declaration of independence as it was a statement about the poker game. Marcus bridled but remained silent, waiting to see how far Sam was prepared to go. Sam responded by rubbing Simon's stomach and fingering the black line of hair which led down into his boxer shorts. Simon's erection lurched forward under the material and Sam smiled at Marcus, almost spitefully.

She then stood in front of Simon to remove her last item of clothing, her knickers.

'Could you help me with these?' she asked, seductively.

'I'd be happy to,' he replied, and he slowly pulled them down, savouring the sight that he had unveiled.

Sam remained standing, naked, in front of him. Using one finger, he traced around her nipples and then down her stomach, not stopping until he reached her clitoris. He suddenly knocked his chair over, knelt on the floor and grabbed Sam's hips so that her vagina was just inches from his face. His tongue darted out and hit its target on the first go. Sam let out a loud groan as his tongue worked her clitoris in a circular fashion. She thought of Danny doing the same thing to her the night before and once again she was aware of the mixture of her juices and Simon's saliva running from her vagina.

Playfully she ruffled his hair while looking across to see Marcus's reaction. But there was nothing. He stared at her blankly and she could see that he had thrown up an impenetrable wall. Sam had beaten him and lost all at the same time. Nonchalantly he shuffled the cards.

'I think it's just us playing now,' he said to John. 'Let's up the stakes.'

Marcus had to give John a nudge to get his attention, as he was transfixed by what was being played out in front of him.

Sam spoke sharply to Marcus. 'I thought you liked watching, Marcus.'

Marcus studiously ignored her and Sam panicked. This had gone too far. She was halfway to being fucked by a complete stranger, something that she was only prepared to do as long as she was sure that Marcus was there to make it safe.

'Marcus, watch me,' she ordered, trying hard to sound confident.

He didn't even look up and something exploded inside Sam. Fuck him, she thought, fuck him because he can't fuck me. Simon was still between her legs, sucking hard on her clitoris, and she put her hand on his shoulder.

'Let's go over to the sofa, it'll be more comfortable,' she said. Simon nodded, greedily licking her juices from his lips.

Sam took command and tore off his boxer shorts as she pushed him on to the sofa. Simon's brown circumcised cock lay stiff against his hairy belly, his balls hanging loosely in their sac. Sam smiled lewdly at him as he grasped his cock, waiting for her to respond. She dropped to her knees and took the head of his penis into her mouth, detecting a faint but not unappealing odour of soap. As she worked on his cock, she bent her head slightly to see the look on Marcus's face. He seemed to be concentrating on the game but Sam felt sure that he was watching from the corner of his eye. She made sure that her performance was perfect.

She knew how to apply just the right amount of pressure with her lips, knowing just when she should bare her teeth to scrape them along the shaft, relaxing her throat when she sensed that he wanted to penetrate deeper. Simon's cock grew thicker towards the base and Sam's lips stretched to take him all in. Simon groaned as she felt her chin touch against the delicate skin of his scrotum.

'Please stop, I'm going to come,' he gasped. 'And I so much want to fuck you.'

Sam let the cock slip out of her mouth. She also wanted him to fuck her. She wanted Marcus to see every last inch of Simon's cock filling up her burning sex. Simon jumped up from the settee and in one move he parted her moist lips and entered her from behind. Holding on to her hips, he brought her back on to his cock with a considerable amount of force. He kept the same pressure up as he fucked her as hard, slamming against her buttocks with his hips. Marcus could no longer pretend to be oblivious and he abandoned the card game.

She threw her head back in abandonment, welcoming each savage thrust.

'Harder,' she shouted, 'as hard as you can.'

Simon complied and his cock tore into her. Age had not impaired his ability one bit. He was fitter than most men half his age and his thrusts were strong and measured.

'Use me,' Sam begged. 'Fill me up.'

As he came, he let out a strangulated yell, not slowing his stroke until he was completely spent. Then he withdrew and flopped back on to the carpet, fondling his still hard penis, rhapsodizing over her beauty. Sam levered herself up so she could sit on the settee, feeling his come oozing out of her battered vagina. Staring at Marcus, taunting him, she dipped her fingers into the juices running down her thighs and plunged four fingers into her aching sex.

Marcus couldn't hold back any longer. He leapt

up from the table and tore off his shirt. He lunged at Sam, digging his nails into her thighs as he shoved them apart and fell on her sex with his mouth. There was no gentleness as he gnawed at her clitoris, driving his tongue deep inside her. The thought that he wanted her so badly that he would lick her out while she was still wet with another man's come drove her wild. But she wasn't prepared to surrender to him.

'You can't fuck me, Marcus,' she taunted him. 'You just can't fuck me.'

As he frenziedly lapped on her clitoris, she felt him trying to ram all of his hand into her but his knuckles prevented him from going any further. The force of his thrusts registered in her whole body and she shook like a rag doll.

'You can't . . .' she started, but orgasm overtook her and she screamed, savagely tearing at Marcus's hair.

There was a long period of quiet afterwards. Marcus sat on the floor next to Simon who was half asleep, still clutching his now softened penis. Sam shivered as she realised that John was still at the table, fumbling with his fly as he leered at her. She curled up into a ball and stared at Marcus, now wanting his reassurance. There was nothing. Sam lay on the sofa clutching her knees, her eyes closed, wondering what exactly had been won and lost that evening.

Chapter Eleven

'COME ON IN, the door's open,' shouted Sam, perched precariously on the top of a ladder.

Judy laughed as she walked into the living room. 'I never thought I'd see the day when Sam Winterton would actually be doing her own decorating.'

'It's very therapeutic,' said Sam defensively. 'And more importantly, it's very cheap. What do you think of the colour?'

Judy admired the sea blue walls. 'It makes the room look completely different, more substantial. But before we get too carried away with the wonders of the Dulux paint chart, how was it with Danny?'

Still at the top of the ladder, Sam dabbed some more paint on to the wall before answering. 'It was fine. He's a nice bloke.'

'So when are you seeing him again?' asked Judy, pleased at the success of her matchmaking.

'I'm not. Damn.' Sam was agitated that some paint had accidentally gone on to the ceiling.

'What do you mean, you're not?'

Sam climbed down the ladder, exasperated. 'I don't want to get into another relationship at the moment. My life's a mess. I haven't got over Toby, I have no job . . .'

Judy interrupted the familiar list. 'Okay, I understand. It might seem too soon to you but you're going to have to let go of Toby.'

'Which is why I'm painting. This place reminds me too much of him. So if you really want me to get over Toby, there's another overall in the cupboard.'

'Couldn't we just go out for a nice lunch?'

'Get changed.'

'I've just had a manicure,' Judy protested, but she put on the other overall. She didn't really mind helping her friend. Clearly Sam could do with some assistance: she'd managed to get as much paint over herself as she had on the walls.

'Don't you think it would have been easier if you had moved the furniture out of the room first?' suggested Judy.

'Well, I thought about it but I couldn't quite balance a three-seater sofa on my back.'

'Sorry,' mouthed Judy, pouring some paint into a roller tray.

'You know, this was meant to be a positive exercise in moving my life forward. But things like not being able to shift the furniture by myself just underline the fact that I'm on my own.'

Judy could see that she had her work cut out for her. It was obviously one of Sam's down days. It was strange how the tables had been turned. It had been a long time since she'd seen Sam so unsure of herself. Normally it was Sam offering words of consolation as Judy cried into her gin.

But Judy always bounced back pretty quickly, normally by bouncing right into another bed.

'So were you and Danny sexually compatible?' she asked, as a subtle way of bringing the topic back up.

'Right down to the same bra size.'

'You mean he's . . .' Judy gasped. Then she twigged. 'You're winding me up, aren't you?'

'Jude, I just need some time. Your roll-on roll-off coping strategy doesn't really work for me.'

Judy scowled. 'You've missed a bit.'

For an hour, the two women painted in silence, Judy trying to correct the many mistakes Sam had made.

'Shit, I've lost another nail,' said Judy eventually, looking into the paint tray. 'I think it's time for a tea break.'

Sam went into the kitchen trailing paint behind her and returned with two mugs of tea. Judy had wedged herself on to the step ladder and was looking at her fingernails with disgust. 'I don't know how Jocasta Innes does it,' she said, as Sam handed her a mug. She blew on the hot liquid and added, 'The other night Alan took me to see that film about Arthur Miller and Anaïs Nin. Oh, and what was the other woman called?'

'June,' said Sam, trying to keep a straight face. 'As in "*Henry* and June." Ring any bells?'

'It was quite sexy,' said Judy, missing the point. 'Though I'm not too sure that I could have a threesome with Alan and another woman.'

'Not if the other woman had bigger breasts than you, eh?'

'Too right,' laughed Judy. 'Oh,' she said, as it slowly dawned on her, 'it's *Henry* Miller, isn't it?'

207

Just then the phone rang. Unfortunately, Sam didn't know where she'd put it. The two women ran around the room, frantically lifting dust sheets and cushions. Sam finally found it under a stack of her framed photographs.

'Perhaps it's Toby,' said Judy, as Sam lifted the receiver.

'Hello?' said the male caller and for a split second Sam thought that Judy might just be right. 'It's Alan. Is Judy there?'

Sam handed the phone, now smeared with blue paint, over to Judy and tried not to feel envious at how happy her friend looked.

Judy whispered and giggled for a few minutes then put the phone down. 'Sam, do you mind if I go quite soon? Alan's got some tickets for a play.'

'It's not Henry Miller's *The Crucible*, is it?' asked Sam.

She laughed as she said it but Judy could tell that Sam was sinking into despondency again. 'You could come with us. I'm sure we could get another ticket.'

'I've got too much to do. By the next time you see it, this flat will be completely transformed.' She didn't sound very convincing.

Judy took off her overalls, cursing the fact that she had got paint in her hair. When she had gone Sam collapsed on to her sofa, noticing that she'd managed to get paint on that too. It was hopeless. She was making a complete mess of things. She was angry with herself for that split second when she'd believed that it was Toby on the phone. She held her head in her hands, feeling the smears of paint on her cheeks.

'I hate him,' she said out loud, but she knew in

her heart that she didn't.

'We're going to the races at Kempton. That should cheer you up,' said Marcus. 'Although it might help if you got the paint off your face first.'

He took out a handkerchief, spat on it and gave her nose a hard rub.

'Ow, stop fussing,' said Sam huffily. 'I'll make sure I'm presentable. Is it a top hat and tails job?'

Marcus nodded.

'I'll have to go out and shoplift a tiara then.'

Smiling, Marcus told her to use the Amex he'd given her. It was as if the evening with Simon had never happened. Marcus had made no reference to it and showed no signs that he was upset by what had occurred. Sam was glad. Everything else in her life seemed to be ruined and if she didn't have Marcus as an escape route she wasn't sure how she'd get through her days.

Having only one afternoon to shop seemed hopelessly inadequate, and to top it off, Judy wasn't available to accompany her. Still, she consoled herself in Browns and soon had an outfit that would knock 'em dead even at Ascot.

The morning of the races Sam spent hours getting ready. Most of that time was spent in the bath trying to scrub off every last trace of blue paint with a nail brush and her skin was raw by the time she succeeded completely. She then put on her make-up and arranged her hair in a French pleat. The dress she had bought was perfect for a summer day in the country. It was a pale green, linen shift dress, its simplicity belying its exorbitant price. The hat, on the other hand, was anything but simple. A swirled taffeta confection in a darker green than the dress, its brim was so wide it threw Sam's face into shadow. She felt the whole look was very Audrey Hepburn. By the time Marcus arrived to collect her she had just about finished, having finally located a pair of white gloves.

She walked to the car, confident that she had got the look just so. Marcus opened the door for her and the expression on his face confirmed what she felt.

'You're a chameleon,' he said admiringly. 'You're always dressed exactly right for the part.'

'Even the East End tart look?' asked Sam, referring to the other night in the pub.

'Especially the East End tart look,' said Marcus, squeezing her knee as she climbed in beside him.

Sam could feel the warmth he exuded. There were going to be no recriminations about the way she'd taunted him with Simon. She made a joke just to be sure.

'Well, I'm all dolled up today and I hope any forfeit you have in mind doesn't involve some stable boy getting manure on the taffeta,' she said, touching her hat.

'That's not a problem, is it?' laughed Marcus.

On the journey they talked about the races and Marcus admitted that he had a couple of horses running, although he wouldn't tell Sam their names.

'I don't want you to know which ones I'm betting on – you'll have to read up on their form. By the way, did I tell you Harriet is going to be there?'

'No you didn't,' said Sam, hitting Marcus with her white gloves. 'Will she be with us?'

'The minute she's finished with the stable boy. Manure on the taffeta notwithstanding.'

Sam sat back, quiet for a while, sipping on the inevitable glass of champagne that Marcus had produced as soon as she had got into the car. She remembered the last time she had been with Harriet and hoped that whatever the afternoon entailed, Harriet would in some way be involved. Marcus was engrossed in studying the form so she watched over his shoulder where he was marking in the hope of getting some hints. He suddenly looked up and Sam felt as though she'd been caught cheating at school.

'Naughty, naughty,' he reprimanded, folding his paper. 'It's too late now anyway, we're here.'

Sam soon found herself in a marquee being plied with yet more champagne.

'At this rate I'm not even going to be able to see the horses, let alone work out the form,' she said, knocking back the champagne anyway.

'Are you still sober enough to see the magnificent filly who's just galloped into the paddock?' asked Marcus, pointing to the entrance of the tent.

It was Harriet. Sam took a deep breath and walked over to her. As usual, Harriet looked stunning. She was wearing a cream two-piece, her head bare with her lovely long, auburn curls left to stray over her back and shoulders. Both women took a step back to admire each other and then embraced.

Harriet flicked Sam's ear with her tongue. 'I'll give you a warmer hello later.'

Sam gave her a lazy sexual smile in return. 'Promises, promises.'

Marcus interrupted them. 'Come on, ladies, there's serious business at hand. Harriet, who are you choosing in the first race?'

'Jockeys or horses?' said Harriet, looking quickly down the list. 'Make it Hobson's Choice at 11-4. The jockey's wearing purple, which doesn't really suit him, but he's got a bum you could crack walnuts with.'

Sam didn't have a clue. How did I ever end up working with figures? she wondered as she desperately tried to work out if 6-4 was better than 7-2. Already she felt tipsy and decided that she would just have to close her eyes and pick a horse at random. She turned her back on Marcus and Harriet and picked. She opened her eyes and saw that she had chosen a horse in the wrong race. On her second pick she chose the date at the top of the paper. Finally, on her third go, she came up with Big Ben.

Marcus seemed surprised. 'He's a complete outsider. Pretty much untested. Are you sure that's who you want?'

Sam wasn't sure of anything. 'I always go for the underdog.'

Marcus went off to place the bets.

'You picked that with your eyes closed,' said Harriet. 'More champagne?'

Sam might just as well have chosen a horse in a different race, as Big Ben didn't even get out of the starting gate. Hobson's Choice won and Sam soon realised that this was one of Marcus's horses when he went off with Harriet to collect their winnings and make the bet on the next race. Sam dropped all pretence of knowing what she was doing and told them she would bet on the same horse as them.

When Marcus and Harriet returned they brought with them the jockey who had ridden Hobson's Choice. Marcus was in earnest conversation with the rider about the whys and wherefores of the race. Sam watched the tiny man and hoped he was nothing to do with any forfeit she might have to pay. She'd suffocate him.

'We've all bet on Shining Light,' said Marcus, when the jockey had gone, ignoring Sam's questioning look.

A roar went up in the crowd and the second race was on.

'Come on, come on,' screamed Harriet, banging her clutchbag on the fence in front of her.

For the first quarter of the race, Shining Light led, but on the first bend the horse fell forward and the jockey came flying off. Marcus looked shocked.

'Excuse me, I've got to go and see that they're both all right.'

Harriet and Sam looked on anxiously as Marcus ran over to the horse and its rider. Both women were relieved when in the distance, Marcus gave the thumbs up signal. They watched the horse being led away, limping badly, before turning to each other.

'Are you here as part of Marcus's plan for me today?' asked Sam.

'Only to make sure that the horse doesn't bite.'

Sam was wide-eyed. 'Marcus wouldn't dare.'

'Oh, it's fine. But you do have to use a hell of a lot of saddle soap.'

'Harriet, you're disgusting.' Sam laughed uproariously. 'Have you got a sugar lump in your handbag?'

Marcus returned and assured them that the jockey was fine, if a little dazed, and that the horse was being checked out by Marcus's own vet. For the next couple of races, Sam went back to choosing her horses blind but again her method failed. She thought Harriet and Marcus must be in cahoots because they picked the winner in both races.

For the final race Sam chose the horse on its name, Goddess, not even bothering to look at the odds. The race started. Goddess was first out of the starting gates and kept up a convincing lead for the first furlong. Then the horse seemed to tire and dropped back into the main body of runners, but as the horses turned into the final straight, Goddess galloped forward in a final surge. Sam screamed encouragement as Goddess thundered across the line, winning only by a head. Sam checked the odds again. They were 20-1 and she quickly calculated how much her five hundred pounds wager had netted her.

She turned to Marcus looking extremely pleased with herself.

'Well done,' he said, giving her her betting slip. 'But it was only one race out of five. I think you owe me something.'

Sam looked at him and then Harriet, waiting to see if either of them intended to let slip the nature of her forfeit, but both of them remaining tight-lipped.

'Just let me collect my winnings,' she said, thinking of how she could now afford to get a professional in to decorate her living room.

'Hold on, I've got something for you,' said Harriet, holding out her hand. It was a sugar lump.

In the limousine, Sam counted out her winnings carefully, much to Marcus's amusement.

'Don't laugh,' she said. 'I'm going to hire an interior decorator. I've spent two days of hell at the top of a step ladder and for some strange reason I've now got a false nail stuck with paint to the wall.'

Harriet shrieked and cuddled Sam. 'And you think that doesn't happen when you hire an interior decorator?'

Sam half hoped that Harriet would again initiate sex in the car but their journey was surprisingly chaste. As the surrounding countryside became more familiar Sam realised that they were on their way to Marcus's house. Pretty soon they were pulling up in the drive and Marcus explained that he wanted to check the stables to see if any of his horses had arrived back yet.

The three of them walked arm in arm through Marcus's formal gardens, chatting amiably about nothing in particular. They passed through a gateway on to the farm land beyond and Marcus took them to the stables. There, Shining Light was being led out of a horsebox by the vet. Marcus spoke to him and he confirmed that in a couple of weeks the injured horse would be as fit as ever. Marcus tenderly patted the horse on its nose.

'There boy,' he said softly, putting his arms around the horse's neck, 'you're going to be all right.'

Once Shining Light was settled in his stall and the vet had gone, Marcus walked to the other end of the stables, beckoning for Sam and Harriet to follow. The other end opened up into a barn-like area where fresh bales of hay were stacked up high. Sam noticed that one bale on the ground had a gingham tablecloth over it. On top of that, sat a silver tray with four glasses and an ice bucket containing their fourth or fifth bottle of champagne that day – Sam had lost count.

'Don't you people drink anything else?' she asked.

'Harriet has been known to drink lighter fuel,' said Marcus, popping open the bottle.

Sam looked around to see that Harriet had climbed on to a bale and was taking her shoes off.

'I only did it once,' she said, aiming a thousand pounds' worth of footwear at Marcus's head.

'Wasn't it when you were screwing that fire eater?' Marcus laughed as the shoe flew past his ear.

Harriet climbed further and disappeared through a trap door in the ceiling.

Marcus handed Sam a drink. 'It's such a lovely afternoon. I thought we'd have some fun out here.'

'There's an extra glass, Marcus,' said Sam. 'Are we expecting company?'

'That's for Shining Light,' shouted Harriet from above as her bra sailed through the air. 'The horse absolutely refuses to drink out of a trough.'

'I think Harriet's waiting for us,' said Marcus, ignoring Sam's question.

Sam took off her shoes and climbed a ladder into the loft. Marcus followed her, carefully balancing the tray with one hand. Hay was scattered around the wooden floor of the loft and Harriet sat naked on a bale, fingering her vagina, a piece of straw between her teeth.

216

'Why Muzz Winterton, that's a mighty purty hat yer wuring,' said Harriet. Then switching accents, 'But I do think it's just a little bit too "town" for a hayloft.'

Sam threw the hat on the floor. As Marcus watched, Harriet stood up and helped Sam unzip the back of her dress, pulling it off her shoulders and down over her slender hips. Harriet turned Sam around and gave her body a long, admiring gaze, cupping her hands under Sam's breasts.

'She's so beautiful,' Harriet said to Marcus, before ripping off Sam's bra and teasing her nipples with her tongue.

Sam wanted Harriet's tongue in other places and stopped her for a second so that she could take off her own knickers. Once naked, she lay down in the hay and spread her legs. Harriet took the hint and fell on Sam's vagina in a frenzy. They switched positions and it was Harriet's turn to lie back with her legs splayed. Sam dived between her legs, savouring the sweet, salty taste of Harriet's wetness as she pushed her tongue deeper and deeper into her, coming out occasionally to flutter over Harriet's clitoris. As Sam buried her face further, she could feel Harriet's wetness spreading across her face.

'That looks like fun. Perhaps I could join in?'

Sam froze, unable to turn around. She'd waited so long to hear that voice again. And now he was standing behind her, watching her roll around naked on the floor with another woman. Shame flooded through her body. The man whom she had loved more deeply than any other was standing behind her looking at the juices that ran down her thighs from her exposed sex as she carried out the bidding of Marcus McLeod. She had let herself become Marcus McLeod's whore and he had brought Toby here to witness the way she had debased herself.

She lifted herself up from between Harriet's legs and turned around, stunned into incomprehending silence. Tenderly Harriet put her arms around Sam's shoulders but Sam shrugged them off. She looked up at Toby, straight into his wonderful green eyes. She couldn't believe this was happening to her. They were all laughing. Laughing at her. Tears stung her eyes and her head swam. It was Marcus's doing. The bastard had brought Toby here to punish her for the way she had treated him at Simon's house. For the way she had showed him up for the impotent fool he was in Las Vegas. He couldn't have her and now he was making sure that Toby wouldn't want her either.

The laughter grew louder.

'Darling Sam,' said Toby, raising the fourth glass of champagne. 'Haven't you realised yet? I'm your last forfeit.'

Sam stared at him, completely bewildered.

'Marcus has told me everything. I'm glad that he's looked after you so well. As Harriet said, you look so beautiful.'

With that, he came over and kissed her full on her mouth, which was still wet from Harriet's sex.

'I've missed you so much,' he said. 'I love you.'

Sam could feel tears on her cheeks. Standing up, she felt as if she was in a dream. How did Toby get here? And how could it be that he didn't mind what had happened in his absence? She had so many questions to ask but Toby silenced her by kissing her again, this time with a more urgent passion.

'Mmm. I love this taste,' he said, letting go of Sam and moving towards Harriet who still lay with her wet vagina displayed invitingly.

'May I?' he asked, as he bent forward, ready to kiss her sex.

Harriet nodded.

Sam watched on in disbelief as Toby began to lick Harriet's lips, playfully taking each one into his mouth and then licking up through her wet crevice to her clitoris. Once again she was enthralled by the line of his muscles, rippling beneath his shirt, the soft burr of his voice, his blond fringe falling across his face. This was her Toby and he was between the legs of another woman. Sam watched as a look of ecstasy spread across Harriet's face.

'He's everything you said he was,' said Harriet, running her fingers through Toby's hair.

Toby urged her to come closer. Still dazed, she edged forward so that she could clearly see Harriet's sex, spread and glistening from Toby's tongue. Toby stood up and began taking his clothes off. Sam was torn between watching him and attending to Harriet's beckoning sex. Harriet made the choice for her, bringing Sam's head down between her legs. Sam licked her clitoris and finger fucked her until she could sense from Harriet's breathing that she was close to orgasm.

'Stop.'

Sam did as she was told. There was a surprising sternness in Toby's voice.

'She's ready for me now,' he said, gently elbowing Sam to one side.

Sam watched, mesmerised by the familiar sight of Toby's long straight cock, shocked that she was so excited at the thought of seeing her lover fuck another woman. In an instant she understood the pleasure Marcus must have drawn from their adventures. She looked up at the millionaire, who was now taking his clothes off. He smiled and nodded, as if to acknowledge her thoughts.

Harriet held her own legs wide apart so that Toby could just ram his cock into her without any interference. In one movement he was driving it into her as far as it would go and Harriet let out a small cry. Sam watched from behind, transfixed as Toby's taut buttocks rose and fell over Harriet. She rubbed her own clitoris and reached out with her other hand to cup Toby's balls. She weighed them in her palm, moving with his body as he fucked Harriet.

'Are you feeling left out?' he asked Sam, as he thrust between Harriet's thighs.

Sam felt a twinge of jealousy. She had dreamed about Toby fucking her for so long and now when she had his cock just within reach it was sliding into another woman. But, she reasoned with herself, there wasn't another woman in the world whom she'd want to share Toby with more than Harriet. She looked at Harriet and then felt compelled to kiss her, relishing the softness of her mouth. Then as Toby increased the urgency of his speed, she straddled Harriet's head and lowered herself until her throbbing vagina made contact with the other woman's mouth. Expertly, Harriet's tongue found Sam's moist opening. Sam leant forward and kissed Toby with ferocity.

'Sorry, Harriet, but I think it's my turn now,'

she said, shoving Toby so that he fell back on to his knees.

She made Toby lie on his back, noticing that Marcus was now enthusiastically rubbing his own engorged penis. She told Toby to open his legs wide. He did as he was told, although the expression on his face showed that he was surprised at this new forcefulness in Sam. At first she just licked up and down his shaft and used her lips to manipulate his foreskin, saying she loved the way his cock tasted of Harriet. Then, as she had done with Danny, she let her tongue trace its way down his perineum and on to his anus.

'Sam!' he said, in a shocked voice.

Sam smiled at him. 'Be quiet and do as you're told.'

She lifted his legs higher so that she could work her tongue further into him. She could see it was driving him mad. His cock twitched and he rocked himself towards Sam's mouth. She decided he needed greater stimulation and she worked her forefinger into his now wet anus. Toby was in a frenzy, begging Sam to fuck him, promising that he would do anything and everything she wanted for ever. Sam laughed and stopped what she was doing.

'You can't stop, Sam. Please.'

But Sam was in control. She wanted to show him some of the things she had learned in his absence, how confident she now was about her desires. Three people lay around her, all masturbating, all ready for her to make her next move. She noticed a riding crop hanging on a beam by the ladder. She went over and picked it up, attracted to its bulbous handle which was made from hard leather. She tapped the crop in her hand, looking around to see whom she should satisfy first. Choosing Harriet, she knelt before her friend and used the handle to play around her open, wet orifice. Harriet's eyes taunted her, daring her to fuck her with it. Sam soon acquiesced, slowly pushing it in, watching as it stretched Harriet to her limit.

The men, both wanking furiously, moved closer to get a better view. Harriet's body shook as the instrument jabbed at her insides. Sam wanted Harriet to come, so she placed her mouth over Harriet's pubis and sucked hard. Harriet let out another cry and Sam could tell it wouldn't be long. She used her tongue ruthlessly on Harriet's clitoris all the while fucking her mercilessly with the crop. Harriet was out of control with desire.

'I'm coming,' Harriet screamed.

As she did so, both Marcus and Toby took her words as a cue for their own orgasms, showering Sam in their ejaculate.

Sam rested back on her heels, pleased with her performance and still excited, knowing she hadn't finished. If Toby was still the same man she knew and loved, she felt certain that in five minutes he would be ready again to satisfy her. She waited, watching the others content in their afterglow. When she was sure that Toby was ready again she turned to Harriet and Marcus. 'Do you mind if Toby and I have some time on our own?' she asked.

Harriet was the first to answer. 'Of course not. I don't think I could take much more of this anyway. I'm completely exhausted. Sam, you're fabulous.'

Sam turned to Marcus and could see he was struggling with his emotions. She knew he desperately wanted to stay but at the same realised that now he had brought Toby into the game, things would have to change. Finally, Marcus agreed but asked Sam if he could speak to her privately. Holding her hands he drew her to the other side of the loft.

He spoke quietly, stroking her hair. 'I know this is the end of our game and I think it's safe to say that both of us have had a lot of fun. But I just wanted to explain what happened between us and why I could never make love to you.'

'Marcus, you don't have to say anything,' she said, embracing him.

'You know that I love you, Sam. More than any other woman I've known. Unfortunately, loving you has left me unable to make love to you. It's my problem, not yours. I realised that night at Simon's that I was only tormenting you, leading you to think that there was something wrong with you. I've put you through hell at times and I'm sorry.'

'But Marcus, so much of it has been good,' said Sam, close to tears again, realising that an important part of her life was coming to a close.

'Nevertheless, when Toby appeared, you looked at me with such hatred. I knew what you were thinking.'

'I was so confused.'

'I know, and it was my fault. But I brought Toby here because I wanted to make you happy. There was no other motive.'

Sam felt ashamed of herself. It was true. Looking back, everything Marcus had done, he

223

had done to make her happy. She had let her mind run away with itself at times. She hugged Marcus tightly.

'It's been a beautiful summer, hasn't it?' he said and she realised he was moving away from her. 'I think somebody's waiting for you.'

She looked around to see Toby, sitting on the floor smiling at her. Harriet was now gone.

'Thank you, Marcus,' she said, kissing him on the cheek.

Marcus left and she felt an intense mixture of sadness and joy. As one door closes, another opens, she thought, looking at Toby. His cock was stiffening again. She walked over to him, smiling, thinking of how she would show him all the things she had learnt this summer with Marcus McLeod.

Chapter Twelve

TOBY LAY BACK on his elbows, his cock hardening appreciatively.

'I've waited so long for this moment,' said Sam.

She heard the stable door bang below her and she assumed that it was Marcus leaving. Then it happened again, louder this time. The banging kept up until she could no longer hear herself think. Toby was saying something to her but his voice was drowned out by the noise. She put her hands over her ears and closed her eyes, wishing the noise away.

When she opened them again, she was staring at a bare blue wall. It was growing dark outside and she had wasted another evening indulging in yet another futile fantasy. Then she heard the banging again. There was somebody at her door. Still in her overalls, she jumped up from the sofa, kicking over a tin of paint on the floor as she did so.

'Damn,' she shouted, lunging for the tin and righting it, a little too late to prevent most of its contents from spreading across the floor. 'I'm coming, I'm coming.'

Her hands were completely covered with paint and she struggled to open the door with her elbow. The banging grew more insistent.

'Would you bloody well wait a second,' she shouted, finally freeing the catch and nudging open the door.

Her mouth dropped open when she saw the man standing out in the hallway. He held out an enormous bunch of flowers, and those unmistakably green eyes creased as his face broke into a huge smile.

'Hello, Sam,' said Toby softly.

Sam slammed the door in his face, leaving a blue handprint just above the catch. Leaning with her back against the door, she tried to catch her breath and calm down. Toby rapped on the door.

'Sam. Are you okay? Open the door.'

Of course she wasn't okay. She was frozen to the spot. She couldn't respond, even if she wanted to.

'Sam, would you let me in?'

This wasn't a dream. Toby was standing out there but she couldn't just let him walk back into her life and hurt her all over again. She didn't want to listen to his excuses, his lies. She had planned this moment over and over again in her mind. She would be cool, detached, aloof. She wanted to show him how well she'd managed, prospered even, without him. And now look at her, spending her days wrapped up in a fantasy because her real life was too awful to contemplate. She was a mess. She couldn't even manage a simple task like painting a couple of walls without making a complete hash of it.

'Sam, your neighbours are watching me. Please open the door.'

In a daze, she relented and Toby walked into her flat, his face reddening with embarrassment.

'Hi,' he said sheepishly, proffering the bunch of flowers.

'How dare you!' she screamed, tears stinging her eyes.

She leapt at him, knocking the flowers from his hand and pummelling his chest, smearing his stone linen jacket with paint. Toby responded swiftly, catching hold of her wrists, letting her struggle until her anger was spent. He held her close as she sobbed uncontrollably.

He took her into the living room and sat her down on the sofa, noticing the paint on the floor.

'I think I'd better clean this up,' he said.

'Leave it!' she spat, holding herself and rocking backwards and forwards.

Toby ignored her and found a cloth. He knelt down, oblivious to the damage he was doing to his suit, and wiped up as best he could. Most of the paint had now sunk beneath the floorboards. Sam simply glared at him. When he'd finished, he stood up and said, calmly, 'I'll run you a bath.'

Sam pulled her knees up under her chin, blazing with anger. But the anger was directed at herself. She was angry at losing her cool, angry at her own incompetence, but most of all angry at how much love she felt for Toby as she watched him on his hands and knees trying to restore some order in her life. She took a deep breath and followed him into the bathroom.

Toby was leaning over the bath adjusting the taps and Sam sat on the edge of the toilet seat.

'Where the hell have you been?' she shouted, instantly hating the shrill sound of her voice. She went on flatly, 'You couldn't even be bothered to phone.'

'I can explain everything.'

'I bet you can.' She was trying desperately hard to hide her bitterness, but her temper was beginning to flare up.

Toby turned off the taps. He seemed completely unfazed by the drama that had just occurred. 'I made the biggest mistake of my life going to Japan.'

'Second biggest. The biggest was coming back here.'

'I'm hoping that's not true.' He looked wounded. 'I lasted three days in Tokyo.'

'Before they found out what a dud they'd hired?' Shut up, she thought, shut up and hear him out.

Toby took no notice. 'After three days there, I told them that I had to take some time off. They weren't too happy about it but they saw that I needed to sort out my commitment to them. I was a big investment for them – it had to be right. But the second I walked out of that office I went straight to the airport and got on a plane to Australia. I flew to Darwin and hired a car. For the last couple of weeks I've just been driving around the Northern Territories, clearing my head.'

He was silent for a while. Was that it? Was that meant to make everything okay again? She had to control herself from leaping at him again.

'Well, I'm glad you had such a nice holiday.' She was seething. 'Haven't they got phones in Alice Springs?'

'I told you, I needed to sort things out. It wasn't about the job, that was perfect. The only thing wrong with it was that you weren't there by my side. I had to make the right decision. If I'd called you, I know what you would have said. I didn't want you telling me that you weren't worth me sacrificing my career.'

What he said was true – she wouldn't have let him quit his job over her. She looked at him, her heart breaking.

'Sam, I'm back,' he said, holding his arms out for her. 'For good.'

Tears began to slip down her cheeks as he took her in his strong arms, kissing her hair, telling her that he loved her. 'Baby, I'm so sorry,' he whispered. 'If you let me I'll make it up to you for the rest of our lives.' He got down on one knee. 'Will you marry me?'

Sam was stunned. This was all too much for her. She said yet another thing she didn't mean. 'Toby, we're going to have to take things slowly, get to know each other again.'

There was an awkward silence until, wiping the tears from her cheeks, Sam caught sight of herself in the mirror. She began to laugh. 'Oh my God, look at the state of me.'

'I'm not looking too good either,' said Toby, glad to have a distraction from the hurt he felt inside.

Both of them were covered in paint. Toby helped her out of her overalls, delighted to see that she was naked underneath. 'Can I share your bath?' he asked, almost shyly.

Sam nodded and soon he too was naked, his long, beautiful cock beginning to stiffen. He climbed in first and Sam slid in between his legs, resting her head on his chest and feeling his erection press against her back. They sat there quietly for a while, Toby smoothing bubbles over her breasts while she stroked his legs, both wanting to take things further, both uncertain of how to play it.

It was Sam who made the first move. Getting out of the bath she towelled herself dry and went into the bedroom, waiting for Toby to follow. When he did, he found her on the bed with her legs spread and her hand on her crotch.

'You don't know how many times I thought about making love to you while I was away,' he whispered, lying beside her, his hand joining hers as it explored her sex.

Sam smiled as she thought of her fantasies over the last few weeks. 'I've thought about you a couple of times. How were those Geisha girls?'

'I was totally celibate,' he said, in a serious voice.

Sam thought of Danny and felt a twinge of guilt. She wondered if she should tell Toby. She didn't want to lie to him. Fortunately he solved the problem for her.

'I don't want to know about what you got up to. I know that as far as you were concerned I was out of the picture.'

He didn't sound totally convinced by what he said and Sam lightly stroked the shaft of his penis to distract him from pursuing the conversation. 'I want to show you what I learnt while you were gone,' she said.

'What do you mean?' he asked sharply.

She realised that his offer of an amnesty regarding other lovers hadn't been quite honest. 'Well, I've had a lot of free time . . .' she teased, then added, 'and I've come up with several new ideas for our list. I've been having a lot of fantasies lately.'

Toby smiled as he remembered the list and Sam didn't want to spoil the moment. She would wait until later before telling him that he would have to write out a new one.

'In one fantasy,' she said, 'I was with two beautiful men. One of them stuck his cock in my mouth while the other licked and fingered my anus. Then they fucked me at the same time, filling me up, front and back. Would you like to watch two men servicing me like that?'

Toby groaned in response, slapping his cock against her leg. Sam then told him all about her striptease fantasy.

'And when I was naked I made three men come up on stage with me. One of them had the biggest penis I'd ever seen. I sucked him off while the other two used dildos and vibrators on me.' Momentarily she stopped her narrative, bent her head and curled her tongue around the end of Toby's penis. 'When I started to come, so did all the men. I could feel it showering over me.'

'Fuck me,' Toby begged.

'You've waited three weeks, a little longer won't hurt,' she said, probing beneath his foreskin. 'Then there was my fantasy about Harriet. She's an absolutely stunning woman I met at a dinner for some TV company. She kind of came on to me. I thought about her a lot afterwards. What it would be like to touch her large breasts. What her vulva would look like, taste like even. I wanted to know how it would feel to fuck another woman with my fingers. I just know that Harriet wanted me to do that to her.'

Before she could continue any further, Toby forced her head down on to his cock. 'I'm telling you to suck it.'

Sam obliged, loving the feel of his engorged member once again in her mouth. She cupped his balls in her hand, thinking about her last fantasy just before he'd knocked on the door. She wondered if he'd appreciate the reality as much as he had enjoyed himself in her mind. She let his penis slip from her mouth and told him how she'd pictured them in the stable with Harriet. 'But I had to drag you away from her,' she said, 'so that I could do this.'

She licked his balls, running her tongue over the coarse hairs, moving down to his perineum. She moistened his anus with her saliva and looked up to see how he was responding. Toby was ecstatic. She dived down again between his thighs and stuck her tongue into his tight opening, her nose nuzzling against the wrinkly skin of his scrotum. She wondered what to show him next.

Her fantasies came back to her in bits and pieces. She remembered her dream about her night at Pain and decided that Danny had just been a try-out for her dominatrix fantasy. She stopped abruptly and jumped off the bed, telling Toby to close his eyes and stay right where he was. Toby complied, eager to know what she had in store. Quickly she shimmied into her black basque, put on her black stilettos and located the riding crop. She climbed on to the bed again and carefully stood astride Toby.

'You can open your eyes now.'

Toby looked up. 'Christ!'

'I always knew I'd find a use for this crop one day,' she said, thwacking the crop against her thigh.

'Be gentle with me,' he pleaded, getting into the role.

'You have to say, "Please, mistress",' she said, swishing the crop very near her lover's testicles.

'Please, mistress.'

Sam sank to her knees so that her labia were only inches away from Toby's lips. 'You want to lick me, don't you?'

'Please, mistress.'

Sam knew that playing the game properly meant making him wait but she, herself, couldn't hold on any longer. She allowed her legs to sink a little further until his tongue made contact with her sex. She had almost forgotten how expertly he performed cunnilingus. Christian in Las Vegas couldn't do any better, she thought to herself.

Toby moved his tongue around her clitoris, only gradually building up the pressure. With his fingers he parted her lips so he could run his tongue along the wet valley and into her sweet-tasting hole. He moaned with the pleasure of once again being so intimate with her. She responded by bearing down on his mouth until his tongue found her clitoris, igniting her body, sending her wild.

She lifted herself off his face, holding herself tantalisingly just out of reach. 'Sit on me,' he said, from between her thighs.

'I'm in charge here, if you remember,' said Sam, tapping his balls lightly with the crop.

'Sorry, mistress,' said Toby, trying to keep a straight face.

Sam stood above him once again. She stretched back her lips, holding herself open, teasing him with the view of her vagina. She squeezed on her clitoris and let her fingers slide into herself. 'I think I need something a little bigger.'

Toby looked up expectantly, waiting for her finally to sit on him.

'A lot bigger,' she said laughing. She reached over and opened her sex toy drawer. 'Remember this?' she asked, removing the twelve-inch dildo.

He smiled. 'Brighton, April the twentieth.'

Sam was impressed with his memory. She bent her knees slightly, so that Toby could see every detail of her wide open vagina. She rubbed the dildo against her glistening entrance then slowly inserted the dildo into herself, putting on a show that Flo would have been envious of.

'This has been my bed partner on many evenings over the last month,' she whispered, her voice husky from arousal. 'One night I fucked myself so hard with it.'

'What were you thinking about?' Toby asked, grasping his cock with his fist.

'About a dinner party,' she laughed.

'Some dinner party!'

'Oh, this one was very special. There were ten people there and I was served for dessert. They stripped me and blindfolded me and one by one they took me, men and women alike. I spread my legs wide for all of them, so exposed, letting them fuck me with whatever came to hand.'

Toby was unable to stop himself masturbating. Sam sensed the struggle he was having with himself, on the one hand, desperately wanting to come but on the other, wanting to wait until he was inside her. She realised how well she understood the workings of his body, knowing just how much longer she could keep tormenting him. For a while she became lost in her own pleasure as the dildo expanded her vagina and she played with her clitoris, bringing herself almost to the point of no return. But it wasn't time yet and she stopped Toby with the heel of her stiletto resting on his testicles.

'Patience,' she said, applying just a little more pressure with her foot.

Toby let go of his aching cock, waiting for her next move. Sam told him about her shaving fantasy, but as with everything she had told Toby so far, she omitted the role Marcus McLeod had played in her dreams. Toby knew Marcus vaguely and as she was due to be meeting the millionaire in a couple of days to discuss his mysterious business proposition, she reasoned that some things were best left unsaid.

'A man covered my pubic hair in shaving foam and then slowly shaved it off. He had to touch my soapy lips continually, pulling them from one side to another while he carefully made sure that I was completely hairless. He made me wear a very short dress and took me out to dinner. Everybody wanted to touch me there. I loved the way my vulva looked bare. You could see every curve and the way I was so obviously turned on.'

'Let me shave you,' said Toby, reaching for his penis again.

She flicked his hand out of the way with the crop. 'Later. The same man arranged for me to have sex with a young market trader while he watched every move that I made from behind a mirror. Then he had me lie on a glass table top so that he could watch from underneath as I was fucked. Wouldn't you like to do that? See another man's cock slide into me as I spread my lips against the glass. So near and yet so far.'

Toby's patience ran out. 'Get down here,' he said, dragging her down next to him.

He took the crop off her and made her kneel on all fours, admiring her buttocks. He parted her cheeks and thumbed her anus. Sam waited for him to penetrate her but instead he brought the crop down on her backside. She wriggled with delight. Toby tapped her again, building up the strokes until the very light lines of red appeared across her creamy white cheeks.

'That's for having dirty thoughts while I've been away. You should be ashamed of yourself.'

'Sorry, master,' she said, happy to have the tables turned on her.

He ran the handle of the crop around the entrance of her sex.

'I think you should be punished by not having sex for a month,' he said.

Sam rotated her hips and the handle slipped effortlessly into her slick opening.

'Oh shit, I can't wait any longer,' he exclaimed, and with that he threw down the crop, grabbed Sam's hips and in one fell swoop impaled her with his raging hard-on. Both of them cried out with the final relief. Sam had tears in her eyes, hardly wanting to believe that Toby, the best lover she had ever had, was back in her bed and wanted to marry her.

Toby shifted her body slightly so she could once again delight in watching their coupling in the mirror on the bedroom wall. Sam looked on, entranced by their joined together bodies. He spread back her labia so that she could watch as he entered her, inch by inch. He had lost none of his skill. While he built up the rhythm of his thrusts, he began rubbing her clitoris. Sam thought she would explode immediately but she struggled to keep control, wanting them to come together.

'Fuck me harder,' she cried.

Toby complied and she soon felt his cock begin to pulsate. She tightened her muscles around his penis to urge him on and to make her orgasm more intense. She waited for his signal. In a final burst, he fucked her harder than she had ever been fucked before.

'I'm coming,' he gasped.

Sam let herself go, savouring the ripples of sheer ecstasy that rolled through her body. Her orgasm was so strong she thought she might faint. She screamed as her body surrendered to the overwhelming sensation, relishing the feeling of Toby's warm come inside her. It seemed to go on for ages until finally they collapsed, as one, on the bed.

A quarter of an hour passed before Toby's half-hard cock slipped out of Sam and she felt their mingled juices gush on to her thigh. Half expecting Toby to fall asleep she was surprised when he jumped up and positioned himself between her legs.

'I haven't finished with you yet,' he said, with a big grin on his face.

He lapped at the juices on her thighs and shoved back her legs so that her knees were pressed against her breasts. Her sex was wide open from the pounding it had taken. Sam held her legs in that position so that Toby's hands would be free to do as they pleased. He burrowed his nose into her vagina, breathing in the intoxicating smell of their lovemaking. Then his tongue set to work spreading her juices, which were now flowing fast and free, and spread them over her anus. Satisfied that the tight ring of flesh was sufficiently lubricated, he slid his index finger in up to the first knuckle.

'Further in,' begged Sam.

Soon the whole of Toby's finger was buried deep. Sam burned with a mixture of pleasure and pain. Keeping his finger twisting in her virgin hole, he used his other hand to attend to her sex. Sam took three of his fingers without a murmur. She felt if he wanted to try, she could probably take his whole hand. But Toby wanted her clitoris in his mouth. Keeping his tongue as stiff as his cock had been earlier, he flicked at the hard nub of flesh until Sam thought this time she really would pass out. Her second orgasm merged into her third. She bucked her hips, bumping her clitoris against Toby's mouth as she came and came until she could barely breathe.

Toby's cock was hard again but Sam had to beg him to take time out for a few minutes.

'There's a bottle of wine in the rack,' she said, lying back against the headboard, stroking her body, still feeling her last orgasm ebbing away. Toby jumped off the bed, saying that her every wish was his command.

'I'll remind you of that in a month's time,' she said, laughing.

He returned with two glasses. Her mouth was parched and she gulped down the cool liquid. They both sat cross-legged on the bed, feeling a warm glow that was more than just sex.

'So it looks like we'll both be down at the job centre then,' said Sam.

'Not at all. Once I realised that I couldn't live without you,' he said, smiling at his own theatricality. 'I contacted some people I knew in London. And yes, they do have telephones in Alice Springs.'

She playfully swiped at his legs.

'And as soon as Samson's heard that I was free, they were begging to take me on.'

A flicker of uncertainty passed across Sam's face.

Toby knew what she was thinking. He became very serious for a moment. 'Sam, if you think that I wouldn't have come back without the job, you're very much mistaken.'

She looked deep into his green eyes and knew he was telling the truth.

'So what about you,' said Toby. 'Any luck?'

Sam braced herself. 'I've got a meeting tomorrow with Marcus McLeod.'

Toby made a face. 'What's he offering you?'

'I'm not quite sure but I don't think it's anything dodgy.'

'Tell him to get lost,' said Toby, thinking that there was nothing that Marcus was involved in that was totally above board. 'Marcus had his chance with you and he screwed it up.'

'But I need to work,' she said.

'You know exactly how I feel about it.' Sam was slightly alarmed by the sternness of Toby's voice.

'Anyway, you've got a job,' he went on more softly, smiling again. 'I told Samson's that I absolutely couldn't work there without my right-hand woman. How would you like to work with me again?'

Sam remembered how it had been when they worked at Walker, Rathbone. She didn't need to be asked twice. 'I'd love to.'

Toby went to fetch the rest of the bottle of wine to toast their new partnership. Sam thought of her dreams about Marcus's offer and how they had kept her going over the last few weeks. She was truly curious to know exactly what the real offer entailed but she agreed with Toby. Marcus had had his chance with her. It would serve her no purpose getting tangled up in his complicated life. Silently she thanked the mysterious millionaire for filling her dreams with such wild thoughts and then put him out of her life forever.

Toby came into the room again and sat on the bed. He kissed her. 'So are you going to give me an answer today?'

Sam pretended she didn't understand what he was talking about.

'I know, you want me on my knees again.'

He knelt in front of Sam and once again asked her to marry him.

'Of course I will,' she said, throwing her arms around his neck, knocking him off balance. They both ended up on the floor and once there Toby lost no time in making love to her again, but this time at a more leisurely, loving pace. There was no hurry and no urgency to finish. They had all the time in the world.

Already published

BACK IN CHARGE
Mariah Greene

A woman in control. Sexy, successful, sure of herself and of what she wants, Andrea King is an ambitious account handler in a top advertising agency. Life seems sweet, as she heads for promotion and enjoys the attentions of her virile young boyfriend.

But strange things are afoot at the agency. A shake-up is ordered, with the key job of Creative Director in the balance. Andrea has her rivals for the post, but when the chance of winning a major new account presents itself, she will go to any lengths to please her client – and herself . . .

0 7515 1276 1

THE DISCIPLINE OF PEARLS
Susan Swann

A mysterious gift, handed to her by a dark and arrogant stranger. Who was he? How did he know so much about her? How did he know her life was crying out for something different? Something . . . exciting, erotic?

The pearl pendant, and the accompanying card bearing an unknown telephone number, propel Marika into a world of uninhibited sexuality, filled with the promise of a desire she had never thought possible. The Discipline of Pearls . . . an exclusive society that speaks to the very core of her sexual being, bringing with it calls to ecstasies she is powerless to ignore, unwilling to resist . . .

0 7515 1277 X

HOTEL APHRODISIA
Dorothy Starr

The luxury hotel of Bouvier Manor nestles near a spring whose mineral water is reputed to have powerful aphrodisiac qualities. Whether this is true or not, Dani Stratton, the hotel's feisty receptionist, finds concentrating on work rather tricky, particularly when the muscularly attractive Mitch is around.

And even as a mysterious consortium threatens to take over the Manor, staff and guests seem quite unable to control their insatiable thirsts . . .

0 7515 1287 7

AROUSING ANNA
Nina Sheridan

Anna had always assumed she was frigid. At least, that's what her husband Paul had always told her – in between telling her to keep still during their weekly fumblings under the covers and playing the field himself during his many business trips.

But one such trip provides the chance that Anna didn't even know she was yearning for. Agreeing to put up a lecturer who is visiting the university where she works, she expects to be host to a dry, elderly academic, and certainly isn't expecting a dashing young Frenchman who immediately speaks to her innermost desires. And, much to her delight and surprise, the vibrant Dominic proves himself able and willing to apply himself to the task of arousing Anna . . .

0 7515 1222 2

THE WOMEN'S CLUB
Vanessa Davies

Sybarites is a health club with a difference. Its owner, Julia Marquis, has introduced a full range of services to guarantee complete satisfaction. For after their saunas and facials the exclusively female members can enjoy an 'intimate' massage from one of the club's expert masseurs.

And now, with the arrival of Grant Delaney, it seems the privileged clientele of the women's club will be getting even better value for their money. This talented masseur can fulfil any woman's erotic dreams.

Except Julia's . . .

0 7515 1343 1

PLAYING THE GAME
Selina Seymour

Kate has had enough. No longer is she prepared to pander to the whims of lovers who don't love her; no longer will she cater for their desires while neglecting her own.

But in reaching this decision Kate makes a startling discovery: the potency of her sexual urge, now given free rein through her willingness to play men at their own game. And it is an urge that doesn't go unnoticed – whether at her chauvinistic City firm, at the château of a new French client, or in performing the duties of a high-class call girl . . .

0 7515 1189 7

A SLAVE TO HIS KISS
Anastasia Dubois

When her twin sister Cassie goes missing in the South of France, Venetia Fellowes knows she must do everything in her power to find her. But in the dusty village of Valazur, where Cassie was last seen, a strange aura of complicity connects those who knew her, heightened by an atmosphere of unrestrained sexuality.

As her fears for Cassie's safety mount, Venetia turns to the one person who might be able to help: the enigmatic Esteban, a study in sexual mystery whose powerful spell demands the ultimate sacrifice . . .

0 7515 1344 X

SATURNALIA
Zara Devereux

Recently widowed, Heather Logan is concerned about her sex-life. Even when married it was plainly unsatisfactory, and now the prospects for sexual fulfilment look decidedly thin.

After consulting a worldly friend, however, Heather takes his advice and checks in to Tostavyn Grange, a private hotel-cum-therapy centre for sexual inhibition. Heather had been warned about their 'unconventional' methods, but after the preliminary session, in which she is brought to a thunderous climax – her first – she is more than willing to complete the course . . .

0 7515 1342 3

DARES
Roxanne Morgan

It began over lunch. Three different women, best friends, decide to spice up their love-lives with a little extra-curricular sex. Shannon is first, accepting the dare of seducing a motorcycle despatch rider – while riding pillion through the streets of London.

The others follow, Nadia and Corey, hesitant at first but soon willing to risk all in the pursuit of new experiences and the heady thrill of trying to out-do each other's increasingly outrageous dares . . .

0 7515 1341 5

SHOPPING AROUND
Mariah Greene

For Karen Taylor, special promotions manager in an upmarket Chelsea department store, choice of product is a luxury she enjoys just as much as her customers.

Richard – virile and vain; Alan – mature and cabinet-minister-sexy; and Maxwell, the androgynous boy supermodel who's fronting her latest campaign. Sooner or later, Karen's going to have to decide between these and others. But when you're shopping around, sampling the goods is half the fun . . .

0 7515 1459 4

INSPIRATION
Stephanie Ash

They were both talented painters, but three years of struggling to make a living from art have taken the edge off Clare's relationship with her boyfriend. The temptation to add a few more colours to her palette seems increasingly attractive – and proves irresistible when she meets the enigmatic and charming Steve.

But their affair is complicated when Steve's beautiful wife asks Clare to paint his portrait as a birthday surprise. Clare is more than happy to suffer for her art – indulging in some passionate studies of her model *and* her client – but when a jealous friend gets involved the situation calls for more intimate inspiration . . .

0 7515 1489 6

DARK SECRET
Marina Anderson

Harriet Radcliffe was bored with her life. At twenty-three, her steady job and safe engagement suddenly seemed very dull. If she was to inject a little excitement into her life, she realised, now was the time to do it.

But the excitement that lay in store was beyond even her wildest ambitions. Answering a job advertisement to assist a world-famous actress, Harriet finds herself plunged into an intense, enclosed world of sexual obsession – playing an unwitting part in a very private drama, but discovering in the process more about her own desires than she had ever dreamed possible . . .

0 7515 1490 X

[ ]	Back in Charge	Mariah Greene	£4.99
[ ]	The Discipline of Pearls	Susan Swann	£4.99
[ ]	Hotel Aphrodisia	Dorothy Starr	£4.99
[ ]	Arousing Anna	Nina Sheridan	£4.99
[ ]	Playing the Game	Selina Seymour	£4.99
[ ]	The Women's Club	Vanessa Davies	£4.99
[ ]	A Slave to His Kiss	Anastasia Dubois	£4.99
[ ]	Saturnalia	Zara Devereux	£4.99
[ ]	Shopping Around	Mariah Greene	£4.99
[ ]	Dares	Roxanne Morgan	£4.99
[ ]	Dark Secret	Marina Anderson	£4.99
[ ]	Inspiration	Stephanie Ash	£4.99
[ ]	Rejuvenating Julia	Nina Sheridan	£4.99
[ ]	The Ritual of Pearls	Susan Swann	£4.99
[ ]	Midnight Starr	Dorothy Starr	£4.99
[ ]	The Pleasure Principle	Emma Allan	£4.99
[ ]	Velvet Touch	Zara Devereux	£4.99
[ ]	Acting it Out	Vanessa Davies	£4.99

X Libris offers an eXciting range of quality titles which can be ordered from the following address:

Little, Brown and Company (UK), P.O. Box 11, Falmouth, Cornwall TR10 9EN

Alternatively you may fax your order to the above address.
FAX No. 01326 317444.

Payments can be made as follows: cheque, postal order (payable to Little, Brown and Company) or by credit cards, Visa/Access. Do not send cash or currency. UK customers and B.F.P.O. please allow £1.00 for postage and packing for the first book, plus 50p for the second book, plus 30p for each additional book up to a maximum charge of £3.00 (7 books plus).

Overseas customers including Ireland please allow £2.00 for the first book plus £1.00 for the second book, plus 50p for each additional book.

NAME (Block Letters) _____

_____

ADDRESS _____

_____

_____

☐ I enclose my remittance for _____

☐ I wish to pay by Access/Visa card

Number _____ Card Expiry Date _____